ALMOST DEAD DRUNK

"Now, let's you and me clarify this matter," Fargo suggested. "You're drunk, so think careful now: was that remark an insult or just some cracker-barrel wit?"

"You can't figure it out, buckskins?"

"I just did," Fargo replied as he set his heels hard and side-hammered the man viciously with his right fist. Smedley's nose broke with an audible snap that made him wince.

Fur boy staggered back and dropped to his knees, blood and snot smearing his upper lip. For a moment his hand twitched in the direction of his knife, then stopped when he saw the less fancy but no less lethal toothpick gripped in Fargo's fist.

"Bother anybody you want to," Fargo said, "except me. If you weren't so corned you'd be dead right now. You've had your one break. If you even get close to me again, I'll gut you."

THE TRAILSMAN
#395

BLACK HILLS DEATHBLOW

by

Jon Sharpe

A SIGNET BOOK

SIGNET
Published by the Penguin Group
Penguin Group (USA) LLC, 375 Hudson Street,
New York, New York 10014

USA | Canada | UK | Ireland | Australia | New Zealand | India | South Africa | China
penguin.com
A Penguin Random House Company

First published by Signet, an imprint of New American Library,
a division of Penguin Group (USA) LLC

First Printing, August 2014

The first chapter of this book appeared in *Burning Bullets*, the three hundred ninety-fourth volume in this series.

 REGISTERED TRADEMARK—MARCA REGISTRADA

ISBN 978-0-451-46908-3

Printed in the United States of America
10 9 8 7 6 5 4 3 2 1

The Trailsman

Beginnings . . . they bend the tree and they mark the man. Skye Fargo was born when he was eighteen. Terror was his midwife, vengeance his first cry. Killing spawned Skye Fargo, ruthless, cold-blooded murder. Out of the acrid smoke of gunpowder still hanging in the air, he rose, cried out a promise never forgotten.

The Trailsman they began to call him all across the West: searcher, scout, hunter, the man who could see where others only looked, his skills for hire but not his soul, the man who lived each day to the fullest, yet trailed each tomorrow. Skye Fargo, the Trailsman, the seeker who could take the wildness of a land and the wanting of a woman and make them his own.

Black Hills, Dakota Territory, 1860—where Fargo faces enemies on all sides, and the greatest threat of all may be his allies.

1

If the situation wasn't so desperate, Skye, I wouldn't have dispatched a courier to track you down. And if you have one ounce of good sense, you'll tell me to go to blazes. This isn't just another routine contract job: it's a forlorn hope.

Colonel Stanley Durant's ominous note had plagued Fargo like a toothache since riding out of Chamberlain and following the Missouri River northwest toward Fort Pierre. But one ounce of good sense hadn't nearly the buying power of one ounce of gold, and right now Fargo was light in both pockets.

It was late afternoon by the time he rode into Fort Pierre, the clear fall air starting to bite and the light of day taking on that mellow richness just before sunset.

It's a forlorn hope. The description didn't help Fargo's mood. He felt weary from his hair to his heels, his ass saddle sore, his belly pinched from hunger. And his mouth was so dry his tongue felt like a dead leaf stuck to the roof of it.

Fort Pierre, he was sorry to note, hadn't changed much since last time he rode through. A fur-trading post on the Missouri, about one hundred fifty miles east of the Black Hills, it had been purchased a few years back by the U.S. Army. The army had built a dismal garrison above the river, a bonanza for soiled doves, and left the crude frontier trading center intact.

The current trading post was a low, sprawling, one-story structure of cottonwood logs chinked with mud and loopholed for rifles. Fox skins were drying on stretchers outside the door. The westernmost third of the building was a thriving grog-and-flesh shop, and it was here that the Trailsman reined in the Ovaro, swung slowly down and stretched out the trail kinks before he looped the reins around a bark-covered snorting post.

The tall, broad-shouldered, slim-hipped frontiersman was

clad in fringed buckskins, some of the fringes dark with old blood. His weather-bronzed face and short-cropped beard were half in shadow under the brim of a dusty white hat with a bullet hole in the crown. He wore a walnut-gripped, single-action Colt revolver holstered to his shell belt and a long, very consequential Arkansas toothpick in a boot sheath.

When he removed his hat to slap the dust from it, the westering sun ignited alert eyes the deep, bottomless blue of a high-mountain lake.

A water casket squatted at one corner of the building. Fargo lifted the top off and let it dangle by its rope tether while he dipped out a few double handfuls to splash his face. He didn't trust it enough to drink it.

"Maybe some oats tomorrow, old campaigner," he remarked to his stallion as he loosened the cinch and pulled a brass-framed Henry repeating rifle from its saddle scabbard. He looked around for perhaps fifteen seconds before heading into the grog shop.

Fargo paused inside the doorway, letting his eyes adjust to the dark, smoke-choked, foul-smelling interior. It was the only sit-down watering hole between Chamberlain and the Belle Fourche River and crowded with the usual run of hidebound roustabouts and ruffians.

So far nobody had noticed him standing quietly near the door, the Henry dangling muzzle-down from his left hand. But he knew that would likely change before long. Unfortunately for the Trailsman, he had a dangerous and unwanted affliction known as a "reputation," and it wouldn't be long before some drunk-as-a-skunk yahoo decided to measure his dick against that reputation.

When he could make out the room better, Fargo made his way toward the long plank bar.

"Hey-up, Smedley!" he greeted the barkeep.

"Skye Fargo! It's been a coon's age," replied a man so heavy that his face creased under its own weight. "What's yours?"

"Whiskey with a beer posse."

"The beer's got plenty of bubbles left, but it's warm—the icehouse is empty until the first winter harvest comes in."

"Warm beer's all right—that'll draw nappy."

From the corner of his right eye Fargo saw that a burly, belligerent-looking drunk wrapped in moth-eaten pelts was watching him with unblinking, trouble-seeking eyes.

Fargo chose to ignore him, casting his gaze around the fly-blown doggery. It was a typical frontier establishment: shoddy-board walls nailed to the logs to help hold the stove heat in, and an uneven floor with several tin spittoons, all but one tipped over. The bullet-holed roof was made of flattened-out cans that had once served for shipping oysters.

The place had the stale, rancid stench of unwashed bodies and cheap popskull. Yet, in Fargo's experience, it was as permanent and elegant as anything else the sprawling and dangerous Dakota Territory had to offer.

Smedley plunked down a shot glass and a chipped beer mug sporting a billowy head. The pelt-clad drunk standing to Fargo's right poked his elbow into a companion's ribs and said something Fargo didn't hear above the raucous din. Both men snickered.

"On the house, damn you," Smedley said when he saw Fargo counting out the last of his five-cent shinplasters. "You go through that routine every time you're broke. You know nobody wants that damn paper money, and that's why you carry it."

Fargo, guilty as charged, couldn't suppress a grin. "'Preciate it, old son.'"

Fargo picked up the shot glass between thumb and forefinger and peered into it. It was said that safe liquor always reflected a man's eye back. This stuff was like staring into river-bottom mud.

"There's no such thing as ugly women or bad whiskey." Fargo rallied himself before he tossed back the shot and shuddered violently.

"Son of a *bitch*," he told Smedley. "Ain't you got white man's whiskey?"

"That corpse reviver will make a man outta you, Skye. Whatever don't kill you can only make you stronger, anh?"

Fargo quickly chased the potent concoction with half of the beer. The burly hard case to his right moved in a little closer to Fargo. Fargo didn't spot a firearm in all that tattered fur, but a fifteen-inch, nickel-plated bowie knife protruded from his red sash like an angry serpent.

"My pard here tells me you're Skye Fargo, the jasper some call the Trailsman," he remarked in a hoarse voice laced with scorn. "Might that be the truth?"

"It just might be," Fargo replied amiably. He was starting to feel that pleasant floating sensation as the strong liquor kicked in fast on an empty belly.

"Well, I'm a Dutchman! I ain't never met no storybook hero. They say you've cut a wide swath, yes, they do!"

The drunk had raised his voice to attract an audience. Fargo sipped his beer and said nothing. There was no shortage of assholes on the frontier. . . .

"Yessir!" Fur boy charged on. "You're a *mighty* talked-about hombre. But a feller has to wunner 'bout a . . . man with such pretty teeth. 'Specially one that needs to put barley bubbles behind his liquor. Mayhap he belongs back in Vermont running one a them whatchamacallits—one a them dancing schools for young ladies."

"Now, let's you and me clarify this matter," Fargo suggested. "You're drunk, so think careful now: was that remark an insult or just some cracker-barrel wit?"

"You can't figure it out, buckskins?"

"I just did," Fargo replied as he set his heels hard and side-hammered the man viciously with his right fist. Smedley's nose broke with an audible snap that made him wince.

Fur boy staggered back and dropped to his knees, blood and snot smearing his upper lip. For a moment his hand twitched in the direction of his knife, then stopped when he saw the less fancy but no less lethal toothpick gripped in Fargo's fist.

"Bother anybody you want to," Fargo said, "except me. If you weren't so corned you'd be dead right now. You've had your one break. If you even get close to me again, I'll gut you."

There was no bravado in Fargo's voice, just a blunt warning. The unwashed, stinking troublemaker stared at Fargo for a few seconds to save face, then rose and staggered into the middle of the room. He had just been publicly gelded and now, by God, he sought to vent his drunken rage on an easier target.

Fargo watched the humiliated blowhard push his way toward a solitary figure leaning in a dark corner.

"You, red speckles! Didn't I tell you to stay clear of this place? Ain't you got no better place to cough yourself to death?"

4

Fargo watched the accosted man move out of the shadows. "The ass waggeth his ears."

He was dulcet-voiced and confident in the way of a cultured card cheat. Fargo took in a small, thin man who had the preternatural gleam in his eye of a consumptive. There was a morbid, ashen pallor to his skin. Obviously of spare frame even when healthier, he had clearly lost so much weight that his cheekbones protruded, lending a ghoulish cast to his aspect. His dirty corduroy coat seemed to engulf him.

His obvious deterioration, however, didn't distract Fargo's attention from the Colt Navy in a hand-tooled, cutaway leather holster tied low on the man's right thigh—and showing clearly below the coat.

"Listen to this shit!" the drunken bully played to the crowd. "Oh, he's savage as a meat ax, ain't he? Too weak to even fuck a woman, but he's the big he-bull now, hey?"

He yanked the bowie knife out of his sash and showed off the blade. "You know, a couple exter holes in them lungs should help him breathe easier, hey, boys?"

The consumptive's unsteady hand held a pony glass of whiskey. He raised it in a toast. "Here's looking at you—which is why I need this drink, shit-heel."

Fur boy's nose hurt like hell by now, and most of the other men were mocking him. His voice yielded to brute anger.

"Swallow back that insult, you worthless cheese dick! Swallow it back!"

"As Mr. Fargo just tutored you, you should never step in something you can't wipe off. Why don't you stumble along now before I decide to kill you?"

Had Fargo blinked he would have missed it. Fur boy took one step closer, and faster than spit through a trumpet the Colt filled the consumptive's hand and spat red-orange fire.

A neat, small hole appeared in the bully's forehead, a thin worm of blood spurting out of it while a pig's-knuckle-size clot of brain matter blew out the exit hole. Fur boy immediately folded dead to the floor, smacking into it like a bale of newspapers.

"God's trousers!" somebody exclaimed. "*He's* feeling hot pitchforks!"

A few men cheered the entertainment—boredom could be worse than Indian attacks. For Fargo it was just one more unremarkable death among many he had either caused or witnessed: just a second or two of nerve-twitching as the body tried to deny the final, certain fact of its own demise.

The consumptive's gaze caught Fargo's eye and quickly moved on, looking instead at the body.

"Break out the quicklime, Smedley! 'He has gone to seek the Great Perhaps!'"

This little burst of animation inspired laughter but also sent the consumptive into a racking spasm of coughing. When he recovered, his eyes again met Fargo's before he looked away and flipped two dollars in silver—dragging-out money—onto the corpse. He edged outside as more coughs shook his frame.

I don't like this, Fargo thought. He was looking at me for a reason, and nothing good could come of it. Fargo had seen the diseased man's face when those brains went flying, and it had all the bliss of a man taking a woman. He was the kill-crazy type, and in Fargo's experience that was the most dangerous kind. They killed on impulse.

"Welcome to Fort Pierre," Fargo told himself. "Now just keep riding."

2

A salmon-pink seam of sunlight showed in the east when Fargo woke up the next morning. He had made a cold camp the night before in a hawthorn thicket along the bank of the Missouri about a mile downriver from Fort Pierre.

Before he rolled out of his blanket, he simply lay still and listened closely. He heard nothing that didn't belong to the place: the unbroken flow of the river, the scolding of jays and the whistle of bobwhites. He rose and buckled on his gun belt, taking a good squint around in every direction.

He had put the Ovaro on a long tether in good graze next to a backwater. Fargo scrounged up enough driftwood and branches for a fire and boiled a can of coffee, sweetening it with the last of his brown sugar.

Watching carefully for weevils in his food, he sat with his back to a tree and gnawed listlessly on a hunk of stale saleratus bread, dunking it in his coffee to soften it up. The wide Missouri, slate-colored in the first light, quickly changed into its famous emerald green as the sun caught it. Its flow was so massive the current made a noise like nonstop wind gust.

Fargo knew that ramrod-straight Colonel Stanley Durant would already be hard at work. He whistled in the Ovaro and dried the dew off him with an old gunny sack. He checked the stallion for galls or hoof cracks, then tacked him and gigged him northwest even before the mist had burned off the river.

When the bluffs overlooking the military post hove into view, Fargo reined in, arrested by the sight of a man astride a horse atop the bluffs, both of them still as statues.

Fargo tossed the reins forward and dug the army binoculars out of his left saddle pocket. He focused them on the man above.

The horse was a strong, coal black "barb," an Arabian with a thick, rich mane and tail. The man slumped in the saddle, dwarfed by his big horse and the endless sky, was the consumptive Fargo had seen yesterday in Smedley's grog shop.

He remained absolutely still in the saddle except when Fargo saw him suddenly bring a big cloth to his mouth and shake with coughing fits. He gazed down on the military post and seemed deep in thought or perhaps distant remembrance.

Fargo rode on toward the main gate. Unlike many frontier posts in less dangerous sectors, Fort Pierre was now walled with squared-off cottonwood logs and there were manned guard towers at all four corners. More and more tribes in this region were heating the war kettles, and the need for constant garrison protection had cut down on army patrols.

Fargo was recognized at the main gate and rode through unchallenged. The fort, like most he had seen in the West, was a drab affair strung out in a rectangle around a huge, gravel-pocked parade and drill field.

Fargo headed straight for the line of low stables. The stable sergeant, an established admirer of the Ovaro, scooped out a bucket of oats for him.

"The old man's steaming and fretting something fierce," confided the sergeant, who was once with Fargo on a mapping expedition into the Bitterroot Range. "Lately, he can't decide whether he wants to piss or go blind."

"I'm surprised to hear it," Fargo said, tossing his saddle onto a wooden rack. "Colonel Durant always strikes me as the strong-willed, straight-ahead-and-keep-up-the-strut type."

"Them days is gone, Fargo. He's forgetting to eat, keeps missing inspections to brood in his office. Why, my hand to God, this morning a recruit walked right past him without saluting, and Old Fuss and Feathers—I mean, Colonel Durant— didn't even ream him out! That ain't his natural gait."

"No," Fargo agreed, hanging his bridle on a can nailed to the wall.

"You got any idea how's come he sent for you?"

"Nah. Nobody tells me anything until I've accepted the job and inked the contract. But he sure's hell didn't invite me to help decorate for the officers' ball."

"I'll tell the world! If at first you don't succeed, try, try a gun.

If he sent for Skye Fargo, it's no feather-bed job. It's dirty, dangerous, low-down work no sane man would take. Good chance your scalp will end up dangling from some featherhead's coup stick."

Fargo met all that cynical barracks wit with a stoic grin. "You sure are a sunny son of a bitch. Thanks for the oats, Ernie."

"Hey!" the sergeant called out behind him. "What's it cost to fall off a horse?"

"Just one buck," Fargo called back. "And it was no funnier last time you asked."

"So you decided to come?" Stanley Durant greeted Fargo, waving him into a chair in front of the colonel's neat-as-a-pin desk.

Fargo folded into the chair and balanced his hat on one knee. "Yeah, I guess a bad penny always turns up."

Fargo noticed that Durant was gazing out a window toward the river bluffs—and toward the lone, dying man keeping his solitary vigil.

"Who is that?" Fargo demanded.

"A killer. One of the most active. He's commonly called the Missouri Mad Dog."

"Logan Robinson?" Fargo whistled and his face came alive with interest. "Never met him, but I've sure's hell heard of him plenty. Allan Pinkerton told me once it's confirmed that he's killed at least forty men."

"Yes, mostly murders, as I understand it. He's not a gunslinger although he can certainly sling one—he's mostly just a killer, one too smart for the law to convict."

"All right, but what's he doing playing silent sentry on the bluffs? Is he planning to kill somebody here—you, maybe?"

"I rode up there last week and asked him directly about that. He replied, quite cordially, that such a person would already be dead if that were his plan. We had an interesting discussion, but he volunteered nothing else about his motive."

"Yeah? Maybe it's just his good sense giving out—looks to me like he's ready to keel over."

"Did he seem so feeble last night when he blew that buffalo hider to blazes right in front of you?"

"You heard about that, huh? It wasn't that spectacular, just a jerk-and-shoot against a man who wasn't even heeled.

Normally I'd call it murder, but the dead man was flashing a knife and Robinson being sick and all, it was justified."

Fargo suddenly grasped a thread of thought. "Yeah, that was right in front of me, wasn't it? And I had this feeling he was putting on the dog for somebody besides the drunks in the saloon. . . ."

Fargo narrowed his eyes slightly and looked at Durant. "An 'interesting discussion' . . . All right, what's the grift, Colonel?"

"Grift is close," Durant replied, "but graft is the legal term for it. And toss murder and extortion into the mix, too. Skye, I'm going to need you to help me buck the chain of command. And I mean buck it hard."

Colonel Stanley Durant was the West Point model of moral rectitude. He didn't cuss, he didn't drink spirits, he never missed church and was ever faithful to his devoted wife. He was battle-tested and every inch the professional soldier. Fargo knew he honored orders from higher-ups as he did the Ten Commandments.

So if he had decided to disobey an order, Fargo had faith it was an order that *needed* disobeying. He gave the colonel an ironic grin.

"Bucking the chain of command," he replied, "is what makes working for the army fun. It's right up my alley—you know that—and we both know that's why you sent for me."

Durant pushed to his feet a bit slowly and crossed to a huge wall map of the military Department of Dakota. Fargo watched worry suddenly mold his face.

"Skye, what would happen if all the branches of the Lakota Nation suddenly went to war against whites in the Black Hills?"

"You know that answer. It would be a mighty short war, and the Sioux would be doing their scalp dances for a week. They're the best light cavalry on the northern plains and piti-less once they paint."

Durant gave a curt nod, his way of recognizing an un-pleasant truth. "And you know the Cheyennes will grease for war if their Lakota cousins do."

Fargo made an impatient gesture with his free hand. "Col-onel, we're both experienced Indian fighters; you don't need to sell me a bill of goods about how dangerous they are. You saying there's a war kettle on?"

"Let's just say it's being heated but hopefully isn't quite boiling yet."

Fargo leaned forward in the uncomfortable chair. "All due respect, Colonel, but you didn't use to mealy-mouth like a politician."

Durant took the jab without reaction. "Skye, I take it you've heard of the Indian Ring?"

Fargo nodded. "A tribe of back-scratching cousins in Washington City who raise their own private herd of cash cows."

Despite the colonel's troubled face he laughed. "You do know how to cut right down to the bone. They know that huge amounts of money are handled by the War Department and the Indian Bureau, money for reservation allotments and salaries, for Indian schools and such. That means plenty of lucrative contracts, and they make sure they bribe the right people—including enlisted men and officers if necessary—to get most of those contracts."

"Yeah, I've seen their handiwork a few times. You know, how they put big, flat stones between the slabs of allotment bacon and count the weight as meat, that type of deal. I'm no Indian lover, but when it comes to whiteskin government, the tribes got their side of it, too."

Again Durant nodded curtly. "Granted, and no officer who claims to believe in God should sanction this. But it's more dangerous this time, Skye, because a new faction within the Ring is gaining power: the military suppliers."

"Sure," Fargo said, trying not to sound bored. "The bunch that keeps stirring up Indian Fever."

"Precisely. There's plenty of profit in outfitting civilians and the army to fight Indian threats. And we can both describe plenty of genuine Indian threats. But now and then they slow down, which means the Ring likes to hire experts to stir up those threats—and where threats already exist, such as in the Black Hills, the goal is to stir up all-out war."

"Yeah, I spun a few waltzes with one of those experts myself down in the Nations. He was doing his damnedest to stir up a war between Cherokees and some other tribes on the rez."

"Right, and you stopped him."

"Killing a man definitely stops him," Fargo agreed.

"That's why I searched my conscience for days and then sent for you. Skye, are you familiar with the name Stuart Brennan?"

Fargo rolled the name around in his memory. "Doesn't ring a bell."

"No, and that's by his clever design. I wouldn't know the name, either, if I didn't have a loyal nephew working in the War Department. It cannot be proven, of course, that right now Brennan is working directly for a major military-supply baron in Saint Louis."

"I take your drift," Fargo said. "Free guns and free flammable liquor for renegades are his main stock-in-trade. It's old hat for both of us. Look, let's lay out all our cards, Colonel."

Durant nodded. "You first."

"We both know it's the U.S. Army's job, under law, to chase all whites out of the Black Hills. The army has done a piss-poor job of it, partly because they resent such rich land being given to savages, and I can see that side of it, too. But anyhow, the frontier army has mostly failed, and now all you top commanders in the Dakota sector are backing and filling, right? Trying to head off a disaster that could reduce all of you to latrine officers?"

Durant flushed with a mixture of anger and embarrassment. "There's that, yes. But, Skye, you're wrong about the cabal of commanders theory. I'm alone in this, strong in my faith but fearful in my mortal mind."

The urgency in Durant's voice rekindled Fargo's full attention.

"New orders have come down, Skye, from the Secretary of War himself: all patrols into or near the Black Hills are suspended until further notice."

"They give any reason?"

"The usual twaddle-and-bunkum: the stand-down is normal policy intended as a goodwill gesture to the red aboriginals, intended to pacify them—you've heard it before."

Fargo mulled all this. "Everybody knows it's gold that's lured whites into the Black Hills. But except for some fools a while back who actually tried to dig a mine, it's just tin-pan prospectors, not miners."

"The whole area is a tinderbox now," Durant put in. "That's sacred territory to the Sioux—apparently they believe there's a small hole there where First Man came up onto Earth or some primitive nonsense. So far, though, they've mostly just stuck to small vengeance raids and demands for tribute. But the younger braves have been pushing the clan elders for full-out war against white intruders into the area."

"And if there're some white men in cahoots who want a massacre of palefaces . . ." Fargo trailed off as the possible outcome impressed him.

"If Brennan can drive this deal to war whoops," he continued, "it could blow up into something bigger than Sioux and Cheyennes. There're other tribes like the Arapahoe and Crow in these Dakota ranges and in good fighting fettle. True, some of them war with one another all the time. But they could make common cause, get all danced and tranced up, and kill every man, woman and child in or even near the Black Hills."

"And keep on doing it for years," the colonel added glumly. "Do you think it really could get that bad?"

Fargo shrugged. "Where do lost years go? Sir, you know how notional the red man is. Even the peaceful Pueblos in New Mexico finally got their bellies full and massacred the Spanish. And the Sioux aren't exactly peace-loving by nature."

It had turned into a damp, chilly morning under an overcast sky the color of dirty bathwater. Colonel Durant's mood seemed to match the weather, a common tendency Fargo had noticed on the Great Plains.

"When I told you this situation was a forlorn hope," he told Fargo, "I secretly still had some hope. Now I see it's a fool's errand."

Fargo blew his cheeks out and gave a long, resigned sigh.

"All right, Colonel, you can nix the pity-me pitch—it's a fool's errand, all right, and you've gut-hooked your fool. I didn't expect this to be a cider party. Tell me about Brennan."

Durant quickly suppressed a victory grin. "A hard man and a realist. Brutal and capable and without one shred of human conscience, religious or otherwise. He's almost certainly in the Black Hills now."

"*Almost* certainly?" Fargo repeated dubiously.

"I know, but it's easier to catch a weasel asleep than to keep track of Brennan. But his methods are always the same. He runs things hands-on. He has three lieutenants, you might call them, but draws most of his effectiveness from coercing and controlling renegade factions led by war-hungry hotheads."

"You got names for these three lieutenants?"

"Only one for certain according to my nephew: a ruthless hill man named Jack Stubbs, who has been Brennan's dirt-worker from the beginning of Brennan's career—Brennan started out as a legman and troubleshooter for a ward boss in Manhattan."

"I assume he has a spy here and at other forts," Fargo said, not making it a question. "These 'agents' like to wave a few hundred dollars under a clerk's nose."

"If so," Durant said, "Brennan knows you're coming."

"Yeah, they usually do when the army employs me."

Fargo clapped his hat back on. "There goes the element of surprise. Any advance on wages?"

Durant piled four half eagles on the corner of his desk. "Twenty dollars should satisfy your . . . immediate needs."

Fargo scooped up the gold. "How many troops do I get? I want to handpick . . . Why are you shaking your head?"

"Sorry. No troops. As things stand now, technically speaking, I'm not disobeying my orders. You're *not* working for the army. I'm paying you out of my own pocket and the contract is between us—a verbal contract. You're not a soldier, and you're after white men, not Indians."

"Bully for you and your rulebook. But I'm s'posed to wangle all this by *myself*? Did you get that big idea from reading *Skye Fargo, Frontier Slayer*?"

"I didn't say you'd necessarily be by yourself."

"Who else, then?"

Durant began shuffling papers around on his desk. "I'd rather not say until it's settled. But, Skye, they'll make cheese out of chalk before government ever grows honest. Even *if* we prevail in this, we could both still get the little end of the horn right through our eyeballs. The Ring won't like it—I could be court-martialed and you could end up spending a few years in a military prison."

Fargo's lake-water eyes glittered with suspicion. "T'hell with that chalk-and-cheese speech—*who* is going with me, Colonel?"

"Stop by the enlisted mess for a hot breakfast before you leave," Durant said, ignoring the question. "It's only bean soup and corn bread, though. Supply routes are tempting targets for that light cavalry you mentioned."

Right now bean soup and corn bread sounded like a feast to Fargo. He rose to his feet, noting Durant's refusal to meet his eyes.

But when the colonel sent another speculative glance out the window, Fargo suddenly remembered how Logan Robinson had likewise averted his gaze yesterday.

Fargo groaned aloud. "Colonel, you don't mean . . . Have you been grazing locoweed?"

"Not at all. Now that you've obviously guessed, just keep an open mind. This job isn't about spying or scouting or mapping, Skye—it's all about killing some to save many, many others. Killing, pure and simple, and I'm giving you a killer more effective than ten troopers."

3

Fargo was halfway up the tall river bluff when the sharp, winter-ice-cracking sound of a rifle shot echoed over the river.

The slug snapped past his ear and air-tickled him before it chunked into the grassy slope a few feet ahead of the Ovaro. Fargo was in a lousy defensive position. The grade was too steep for his stallion to end this with a burst of speed. And Fargo sensed there wasn't time to wrestle the Ovaro down flat and hide behind him. His only option was to get as low as possible as quick as possible.

Underscoring his correct decision, the rifle cracked again, the bullet flumping into the tight bedroll tied under the cantle straps. Fargo jerked both feet from the stirrups, snatched the Henry from its boot, and torqued himself out of the saddle, landing in a cat stance and working the Henry's lever.

He smacked the Ovaro's glossy rump as hard as he could, sending the stallion up to the lip of the bluff.

A third shot rang out as Fargo went prone, kicking a plume of grass and dirt into his face. By now he knew the shooter was due west of him. He spotted gray-white powder haze above a juniper thicket.

Even if he could notch the Henry on a target, it was a long and difficult shot from this sloping angle. On level terrain, with good elevation and wind calculations, Fargo could score hits every time out to three hundred yards from the prone position. This ambusher was perhaps just in range.

A fourth shot, this one chewing into the ground so close to his head he felt the concussive power of the big slug burying itself in dirt.

That's likely the last of his ranging shots, Fargo concluded, thinking like his enemy. Without willing them, his muscles tensed in the urgent need for immediate action. This next one could bore him through. . . .

Fargo rolled hard and fast to a new position as the rifle barked again. He lifted his head enough to catch a break: a glimpse of the shooter's partially exposed head and shoulders.

Fargo settled his left elbow, laid his cheek alongside the stock, and carefully lined the sight up with the ambusher's head. Then he raised the muzzle slightly to allow for bullet drift.

He took in a deep breath, let it out slowly. As he paced the exhaled breath evenly he took up the trigger slack in one slow, continuous pull until the Henry kicked into his shoulder.

The angle was tough and he missed. But a dirt geyser shot up from just in front of the thicket, spotting Fargo's next shot for him. The Henry didn't have exceptional knock-down power, but now he put its famous sixteen-shot tube magazine to good use, levering and firing successive shots in a hammering racket.

By the time Fargo's rifle fell silent, a thick, acrid powder haze billowed around him. He rolled again, keeping within the haze, and waited for return fire. But nothing interrupted the silence except the constant, insistent murmur of the Missouri's current.

"You either plugged him or sent him hightailing, Fargo!" called Logan Robinson's weak but pleasant voice from above.

"I haven't heard a horse," Fargo called back.

"Me, either, but that haze is blowing off you."

Fargo made a run for the top of the bluff. He had perhaps fifteen feet to go when a potent blow to the head dropped him in his tracks as if he'd been war-axed.

Fargo felt the sun hot on his face and his eyes blinked open, waking him to pounding, throbbing head pain.

"Too bad, Fargo," Logan Robinson greeted him. "You're going to live."

Fargo's head felt like a bull train had rolled over it. The pain seemed to extend even into the roots of his hair.

"You were careless that time, Fargo."

"I don't believe I put in for any medals. Jesus!"

"It wasn't a graze," Logan explained, standing over Fargo. "It was a solid crease right above your left ear. You've been out for over an hour."

Fargo tried to sit up and scrapped the idea almost immediately, flopping back into the grass and groaning.

"You're missing a small patch of hair, and half of the left side of your face is already a dark bruise."

Fargo tried again and this time managed to sit up. The Ovaro was hobbled nearby and busy taking off the cured grass on the bluff.

"I just roweled Colonel Durant for costing me the element of surprise," he said. "But I didn't think I'd pay for it so damn soon."

"You also just learned lesson number one about Stuart Brennan: don't miscalculate him and *don't* underrate him. No man has stopped him yet, not even me."

"I don't give a shit if he bulled the queen of France," Fargo shot back irritably. "I don't require any lessons about staying alive from you *or* Brennan."

Logan, ashen-faced in the sunlight, waved the rebuke aside. He produced a slim silver flask from beneath his corduroy coat. "Spot of the antifogmatic?"

Fargo shook his head, eliciting more pain.

Logan laughed so hard he went into a fit of coughing. "Won't drink a lunger's spit, eh? Wise man."

"You're wasting your time trying to stir my pity or make me feel guilty. Ain't my fault you're sick. Last time I heard, the death rate is one per person."

Logan raised the flask in toast: "To dark saloons and fair women."

"Why'n't you lay off that shit," Fargo said. "It's not helping your health or your disposition."

"Speaking of fair women," Logan pressed on as if Fargo hadn't spoken, "I dallied once with this pretty little redheaded firecracker back in St. Joe. This sounds like I'm starting a joke, but it's a true story. Well, naturally, being a man, I wanted to go to sleep right after I finished. But I had made the mistake of bursting a ripe maidenhead, and I quickly discovered how virgins can swoon the first time they get a taste of the dirty deed."

Logan tipped the flask again and wiped his mouth with the back of his hand.

"Immediately she went into this flight of romantic fantasy

18

and wouldn't turn off the tap. 'Oh, my precious darling, we are now a part of each other. You are a part of me, and I a part of you.' So all I said was how that was going to make it mighty damn confusing when we tried to get dressed in the morning. Fargo, do you know that miffed little bitch broke a water pitcher over my head?"

"I've heard that one in a dozen saloons. Spare me the river-boat hustle—why do you spend so damn much time up here?" Fargo asked.

"I always drink better when I think."

"That actually makes sense. I must've been creased hard, all right."

"Besides, this is a perfect place for me. Heaven doesn't want me and hell's too good for me. So for now I'm trapped up on this bluff in the real world between, coughing blood into snot rags and feeling death creep into me like winter cold."

"If you're that bad off," Fargo said, "and you sure appear to be, how in the hell can you expect to ride into the Black Hills and pull your freight? Jerking a trigger is only the easy part."

"Durant is a top judge of male stamina, and he has faith in me."

"I can't gainsay that," Fargo conceded. "But why would you want this kind of work in your health? If it's a quick death you're after, you've got a sidearm and the guts to eat it."

"My reason is more mundane than all that. Like you, I find myself in straitened circumstances."

"I guess that means you're broke?"

"Busted, disgusted and can't be trusted. I lied just now about my true reason for doing this job. Robinson is only the name of a family that took me in once. My real name is Logan Brennan."

"This Stuart is your brother?"

"Cain and Abel, yes. But for the time being I'm not at all eager to have that fact paraded around, and I ask you to keep it dark from others."

"And Durant knows this, right?"

The consumptive grinned. "You mean he didn't tell you? Must have slipped his mind."

"Yeah, must have. Look, this is all a mite cloudy and needs clearing."

"The worst sins of all, Fargo, are the ones left uncommitted. I've put it off too long because of the power of ancient taboo—it's time I killed my brother."

"Pile on the agony," Fargo muttered, shaking his head in puzzlement at his own foolish self for the harebrained things he agreed to.

"Don't be fooled by appearances, Fargo. This red-speckled cough of mine has orphaned my hopes, yes, but not my love of bloody mischief. I'm a true-blue, blown-in-the-bottle killer, and my imminent demise hasn't softened me a bit."

"Talk is cheap. There's rough sledding ahead—and it's not just your brother and his lick-fingers. We'll have to keep red john from lifting our hair, and there're scores of illegal prospectors panning Spearfish, Whitewood and Deadwood Creek—since we won't be panning or working a long tom, they're going to see us as gold thieves or hired guns. And I'm sure you know how those boys handle a threat like that."

Logan nodded. "I've cardsharped in some of the roughest places in the West, even Fort Griffin and Virginia City. But I religiously avoid prospecting camps."

"We're gonna be on the move constantly and constantly fatigued. Your courage I can't speak to, but I'd prefer you to stay back because I don't think you can survive the exertion."

"The colonel's already hired me," Logan reminded him.

Fargo shrugged. "I'll bury you when the time comes. I s'pose it's pointless to ask why you mean to kill your own brother?"

"It is, but don't get me wrong. I'm a lot like Stuart. We'd both steal the coppers from a dead man's eyes. The only future we had as kids was grubbing taters on a hardscrabble farm in Missouri. We had differing views on life, and each went our own criminal ways."

A coughing spasm interrupted Logan and he backed up to brace himself against his horse. His tight-lipped smile seemed to cost him an effort.

"But Brother Stu? Unlike me he avoids unnecessary killing. But just *try* to block his profit path and he'll rip a man's heart out with his bare hands. Women, babies, old pensioners—he'll eat them alive because he has no scruples where there's a dollar in it."

For a moment the consumptive had failed to filter the bitterness from his normally ironic tone. And it was in that new tone, not his face or his words: regarding his brother, Logan Brennan had one hell of an ax to grind, and Fargo had no use for it.

"This is a job," Fargo reminded him, "not a grudge match."

"The two can mix well. When do we dust our hocks?"

"Today. As soon as we lay in supplies."

"Good. You're the boss—Durant made that clear. But you just remember my warning about my brother, hear? And that extends to his well-paid toadies—you just missed death by less than an inch, and it will get closer. From here on out, Trailsman, we're both marked for carrion."

"What *I'm* going to remember," Fargo assured him, "is all the men you've shot in the back."

4

Riding due west from Fort Pierre it was about one hundred fifty miles to the creek-rich part of the Black Hills favored by recent prospectors. Fargo knew the breed well as rugged individualists who didn't give a damn what the Indian lovers wanted—there was color in those hills, literally for the picking.

Fargo knew there was nothing even approaching a gold rush going on yet—the Lakota made sure of that, and the U.S. Army had until recently made some effort to keep the larger groups and operations out.

They pushed on steadily but spelled their mounts frequently. The riding was easy most of the time across flat and rolling plains. But Dakota had grown especially tense and dangerous, and Fargo guided constantly by using the Pole Star and Dog Star to keep careful bearings. He held to a route that avoided the riskiest Indian ranges, holding a course north of the Badlands but well south of the Belle Fourche.

The longest stretch of the ride was across mostly open plains. But the sea of frost-browned grass gave way occasionally to wide meadows of faded blue columbine or little hollows sheltered by pines. Fargo always reined wide past the trees.

Toward the end of their journey Fargo pushed harder and paid no attention to day or night, only to keeping the horses reasonably rested and well grained. Mostly the two men rated their horses at a lope, a pace that made good progress without lathering the strong mounts.

"I always try to enter the Black Hills from the south," Fargo remarked at one point when they stopped to water their mounts from a small pond. "Bear Butte guards the north, and the Sioux meet there in conclave."

Logan, Fargo had to admit, had held up well so far considering his condition. He watched the notorious killer, bent against the wind, hands unsteady but competent, shape himself a smoke. But he wasted three matches fighting the wind for a light before he finally gave up.

Fargo shook his head. "Any fool," he remarked to Logan, "could've told you those matches would go right out in this wind."

"Any fool just did."

Twice a day Fargo went through a careful ritual. He first checked the Ovaro's hooves for cracks or stones. Then he checked his saddle and pad for burrs; he carefully examined the cinches, latigos, stirrups; finally he inspected the bridle and reins.

Once, Logan watched him with bemused wonder when Fargo cut a few fringes from his buckskin shirt and used them to mend a weak spot in one of the cinches.

"So those fringes aren't just for show," he said. "Do you rock that horse to sleep, too?"

"Like most killers, you've spent too much time in town," Fargo shot back. "You let a horse founder or tack get ruined in country like this and you're in a world of hurt."

On the third day the Black Hills, an isolated extension of the Rockies, rose clearly before them. Fargo took in a high-altitude island of timber surrounded by level, barren, treeless plain. The hills were far less arid than the surrounding region because some of the peaks rose more than a mile high. Fargo had watched them arrest rain clouds that otherwise quickly blew over the dry plains. The resulting forests and streams made the Black Hills a haven for bears and other wildlife.

And wild rumors about fifteen-pound gold nuggets lured in even more dangerous wildlife, men burning with gold fever.

"Yeah, I see why they're called the Black Hills," a visibly impressed Logan remarked. "It's high noon but they look dark from here."

"Yeah, well, don't forget our problem: they're the *Paha Sapa* to the Sioux," Fargo reminded him. "And if they catch us there, our brains will boil slow over a small fire. Warpath Sioux are no boys to fool with, especially here, and that's why we're not riding in until after dark."

The two men camped in a sheltered copse near a small stream. A fire was out of the question now so they gnawed on cold corn dodgers and dried fruit.

Fargo sat with his back to a boulder and watched the Ovaro stretch his neck toward the little stream to drink. The muscles looked dusty but still sharply defined in the brittle afternoon sunlight.

Logan had stretched out using his saddle as a pillow. "Fargo, you think there's as much gold in the Black Hills as people say?"

"Prob'ly even more than you hear about in the saloon rumors. When a man can ride in with just a knife and pull out thirty dollars a day just from cracks between rocks, you know there's a helluva deep-rock lode someplace."

"If so it won't take the codfish aristocracy long to get control of it."

"I reckon not."

"Reckon? It never fails. My brother is hell unleashed, but he's right: the rich man's always dancing while the poor man plays the fiddle."

Fargo eased his hat lower and said nothing. Logan coughed for about ten seconds.

"Of course that doesn't bother the Trailsman," he said when he recovered. "While the rich man's dancing you're screwing his wife."

"With me it's always the lady's choice," Fargo assured him. "Besides, there's something to be said for knowing how to play a fiddle. Wish I could."

"Look, I saw how things stand even when I was a kid. An *honest* man, Fargo, works his ass off twelve hours a day so he can eke out just enough to keep the wolf from the door—if he even *has* a door. With a marked deck I can make enough legem pone in four hours to match a year of 'honest wages.'"

Fargo tipped his hat back. "Don't peddle that sorry shit to me. You're just making hard work and rich man's greed your excuse for being a criminal. Well, you ain't Robin Hood. A man who puts his mind to it has other choices besides shooting a man in the back."

"I'm so inspired I've got goose bumps. What's next, a temperance lecture?"

Fargo glanced at him. A shaft of sunlight pierced the canopy of branches overhead and illuminated Logan's exhausted, skullish, ashen face. Fargo could still make out the intelligent planes and angles underlying this altered visage. It was the kind of face

women must have considered more interesting than handsome—
a distinction that had probably cost him nothing in his success
with the opposite sex before disease ravaged him.

To Fargo, however, it was the familiar yet hard-to-type face of
a man who made no distinction between killing and murdering,
a man who rejected even the most basic code of honor—a man
who might try to murder him in the blink of an eye.

"You've already made your brag about how much you enjoy
killing," Fargo said, "and you don't deny burning down un-
armed men. It wasn't rich men or hard work that drove you to
become a low-down murderer."

"You'll appreciate my skills before this job is over."

"So you keep telling me. There's no skill but in the doing."

"That's another one I'll have to write down."

When the sun was a round, dull orange ball low in the western
sky, Fargo kicked Logan's foot to wake him.

"Get horsed," Fargo ordered. "We're riding in."

In less than an hour the two horsebackers entered the Black
Hills south of a towering peak that rose well over a mile into
the sky. Fargo knew this region well and followed French
Creek as it twisted and turned, taking them farther into the
tinderbox of the Black Hills.

They moved on slowly, the horses walking, for at least two
hours. Abruptly a savage war cry sounded, somewhere well out
ahead of them in the dense, tree-covered darkness, followed by
a barrage of war whoops and the sudden crackling of gunfire.

"Both sides have repeating weapons," Fargo said. "I recognize Henry rifles and Spencer carbines."

"Of course, my brother's on the job. But I thought the Sioux
never fought after dark?"

"The only thing a Sioux *never* does is make it easy to kill him.
They'll fight at night if their village is attacked—or if they're
corned up on strychnine-laced firewater and following a renegade who doesn't abide by the tribal law-ways. You're right—this
is likely your brother and his men stirring up the shit."

Fargo heard what sounded like white men cursing, more
yipping war cries and crackling gunfire, and eventually silence except for the singsong cadence of millions of insects.

"Sounds like a camp or something out ahead of us," Fargo

said. "We'll bed down right here until sunup. I like to see what I'm riding into."

At first light the two men were advancing on foot leading their horses. A knife-edge of cold lingered in the early-morning air and their breath formed shimmering ghosts. They were moving through forested slopes covered with tall ponderosa pine, spruce and aspen. As the sun inched higher, huge chunks of crystallized gypsum winked at them like mirrors in sunlight.

"This place is something," Logan remarked, visibly impressed. Occasional breaks in the trees revealed ancient granite peaks that had been wind-eroded to odd-shaped spires.

"Yeah, the Sioux think so, too, and they can pop up anywhere. These hills are honeycombed with caves, and ambushes are easy to pull off."

They emerged in a clearing overlooking French Creek.

"You have got to be shitting me," Fargo muttered. "How stupid can they be?"

He had seen small camps around these creeks before, usually just a tent and rarely more than two or three. But this before him, crowding the opposite bank of the creek, was six sorts of trouble.

"No wonder the colonel is having a conniption," Logan said sarcastically. "No schools or churches, I notice."

The budding gold camp had mushroomed into being on a grassy swale between the creek and the edge of a forest behind it. It ranged from a few small but solid cabins to about a dozen crude shacks and she-bangs with small tents interspersed. Several large tents housed enterprises of various kinds.

The heartiest of the gravel-panners had braved the early-morning cold water and were already working their stakes along the creek bed. Others milled around one of the big tents, chewing on bear-sign doughnuts and gulping cups of hot coffee. The tent appeared to be a saloon, eating house and barbershop all on one stick.

This collection of intruders into the Black Hills was a foolish and dangerous undertaking, and Fargo knew death and suffering would likely come from it. But that wasn't what he meant by "stupid."

It was the glaring sight of a dead Sioux warrior mounted on a board and prominently suspended from a high tree branch. He had been castrated and his pecker and sac crammed into his mouth. Crude red letters painted over his head declared: SAFE ON THE REZ AT LAST!!!

"Body looks fresh," Logan remarked with professional boredom. "He must have been dispatched during that ruckus we heard last night."

"They got one day to take that body down," Fargo said, "*maybe*."

"Why a day?"

"A lot of Sioux warriors won't return to a place where a person was killed," Fargo replied, "until a full day and night pass. They figure a vengeful spirit has that long to take over a new body and he can grab anybody."

"You think these clodpolls know that?"

"Couldn't say, but if word of this gets back to the Sioux," Fargo replied, "it's full-out war. The renegades and the tribe loyalists will parley and paint. The tribes disfigure and dishonor enemy dead all the time, but for white men to do this to a Sioux in the middle of their big-medicine mountains . . . These sourdoughs must've been scratching their asses with both hands when brains were passed out. C'mon."

The two men tethered their horses to graze and crossed the creek on a rope-and-plank bridge.

"Fargo! Skye Fargo!"

A friendly-looking man waved at Fargo from a group of prospectors gathered outside the biggest tent. It took Fargo a moment, as he walked in closer, to recall him.

"Jim West!" he called back. "Still chasing the yellow glitter, huh?"

"And catching it, by God! Last time I seen you was out in the Rockies when you cleared them claim jumpers outta Buckskin Joe."

When Fargo was close enough, West caught sight of his bruised face, fading but visible.

"Damn! Mule kick or an anvil?"

Fargo ignored the question and nodded toward the dangling corpse. "Indian trouble last night, I see."

"And how! The red bastards had repeating rifles, too, plenty of 'em. Lucky for us we maintain a night guard and got plenty of firepower. We only had one man wounded."

"I still say this bunch was jo-fired on strong water," said the prospector next to West. "Some of 'em could hardly stay on horseback."

Like West and most of the others he wore sturdy hopsack trousers and a coarse pullover of gray homespun. Standing in water all day was rough on leather, and several of them wore broken boots held together with strips of burlap.

"Yeah, think about that," Fargo said. "All of a sudden they got firewater and repeating rifles . . . and I doubt they found either in a limestone cave."

"You know something about that attack, Skye?" West asked.

Fargo knew plenty, but he wasn't at liberty to divulge details without it eventually getting out that Colonel Stanley Durant had become a loose cannon, possibly even a traitor when the Indian Ring got done with him.

"I know that somebody is stirring up the Indians against you," Fargo replied. "But *that*"—he nodded toward the castrated Sioux—"will wind them up to a fare-thee-well. Jim, you ought to know better than to let a Sioux see a sight like that in these mountains."

"*Let* the sons a' bitches see it!" sounded off a sourdough with a wild red beard. "Let 'em see Chief Blanket Ass there eating his own pizzle! That's why we put the red arab on display—to learn the rest a lesson."

"This ain't the first raid, Skye," West explained. "Feelings is running high. And we *ain't* pulling out yet, the army and the red heathens be damned! Another month and it'll be too damn cold to prospect, and right now most of us are pulling out twenty to thirty dollars a *day*, and using butcher knives to do it! These is poor man's diggings, but they won't stay that way for long. It's make hay while the sun shines."

Fargo gave a weary nod. Most of these prospectors were honest, hardworking men whose farms had failed on the eastern plains and prairies, leaving them and their families destitute. One month panning these Black Hills creeks and they could save those families from starvation for maybe two years. Fargo couldn't blame them for taking the risk, but unless things changed in a puffing hurry, none of them would live to feed those families.

"I ain't telling you boys to pull out," Fargo reasoned. "I know you won't stand for that, and besides, I don't go in for *any* man claiming to own these mountains, red or white. But that"—he nodded toward the body on display—"is nothing but trouble on stilts. This is no magazine story made up by a boardwalker back East—the Indians ain't doomed just because you figure you're superior white men. You'll all soon be up against it hard, and greenhorn tricks like that are just fuel to the fire. You need to rile cool and remember that the readiness is all."

"I wasn't for it, Skye," West said, looking uncomfortable. "But there was a rider through here yesterday, see, and he had some things to say."

Fargo caught on instantly. Ever since he and Logan Brennan had walked in, the men in camp had turned suspicious, not curious. Fargo assumed it was because some had recognized the man they knew as Logan Robinson, the Missouri Mad Dog. But now he realized Stuart Brennan had cold-decked him yet again.

"And this rider," Fargo prompted, "I'll bet he had some uncharitable things to say about me?"

"*And* that fuckin' murderer with you!" Red Beard took over. "This rider said how Skye Fargo had sunk low and throwed in with a back-shooting, skunk-bit mad dog named Logan Robinson. And there he stands beside you looking three days past burying."

Fargo chafed at his orders. Colonel Durant had hoodwinked him into working with Logan, and why wouldn't these men conclude Fargo chose to work with the dregs of criminal society?

"That ain't the half of it," said the man closest to West, a Volcanic repeating rifle cradled in the crook of his left elbow. "He said how you and the back-shooter here has been hired on by some mining barons to get us little fellas run out or killed."

"Jim," Fargo said, "you know me—we fought side by side against high odds at Buckskin Joe. You really think I've hired my guns out to kill you prospectors?"

"No, Jim don't," Red Beard said. "He said so yestiddy."

Red beard brought the twin muzzles of his Greener to bear on Fargo. "But the rest of us don't know you, Fargo, 'cept for this—you're necked to one of the greasiest shit stains in the country, and that's proof enough for me."

5

Fargo watched Red Beard close, especially his nervous hands. He sized the man up as hot-tempered but not experienced at holding a man under the gun—unsure of himself and thus unpredictable.

"I'd advise you to reconsider," Logan spoke up. "All you men are right—I'm a killer. But even devils can do some good in their constant pursuit of evil."

"The hell you babbling?" Red Beard demanded.

"He's saying," Fargo explained, "that this time he's been hired to kill your enemies, not you. And that's the truth, although I can't vouch for his intentions. Sometimes things that stink can be good for your health."

"Fargo's been arrested and such, boys," Jim West put in. "But it's mostly penny-ante stuff like brawling or fornicating on Sunday. I don't know why he's with Robinson, and I don't like it none, either. But maybe good killers are needed."

He looked at Fargo. "But who you working for, Skye—the army?"

Again Fargo chafed at his forced silence. "I know it looks bad for me, Jim, but I can't tell you that. I give all of you my word: I'm not here to drive you out or kill you. I can tell you that outside meddlers are planning to put the Sioux on you full chisel, and we're here to try to stop it."

"Lower that smoke-pole, Clancy," West urged Red Beard. "I'm telling you Fargo's straight grain clear through."

So far Clancy hadn't curled his finger around the triggers, and Fargo figured that's why Logan hadn't killed him. The tension eased considerably when Clancy lowered the Greener. His flash of anger had passed, allowing him to think more clearly.

"I ain't heard of no stain on his name, neither," he admitted, "'cept for siding Robinson. 'Sides, I didn't cotton much to that blowhard 'messenger' that rode through here. There ain't no town criers in these hills—he's got a finger in some pie, and that's how's come he talked agin Fargo like he done."

"Who was this messenger?" Fargo asked.

"I ain't sure he even give us a name. Big, beefy, know-it-all son of a buck, spoke high up in his nose like a hill man."

"Jack Stubbs," Logan told Fargo quietly. "Stuart's master stallion."

The prospectors, knowing time was money, had begun peeling away from the group to work their illegal but profitable claims.

"Let's vamoose," Fargo said. "We jumped over a snake that time, but some of these old boys are suspicious—especially because you're here."

"Let's cut the dust in that bucket shop first," Logan countered. "A sick man has to drink his breakfast every morning."

They ducked inside the largest tent and turned down the biscuits and ham gravy when the cook told them it was a dollar a plate. They settled for a shot of forty-rod—two bits overpriced—drunk from battered tin cups chained to a sawbuck counter.

"When you jump over a snake," Logan spoke up after tossing back his liquor and recovering his breath, "you leave it alive to bite you another time. These prospectors are on the ragged edge, Fargo, and I'm not fooled by Clancy's weepy conversion."

"It'll be a tricky piece of work," Fargo agreed. "Every bit of gold they've pulled out of that creek is carried right on them or hidden close by. They're jumpy and hair-trigger and gold-feverish, and that will get worse when the attacks against them get better organized and they don't. Hell, they won't even trust one another if they still do."

They were halfway back to the swaying bridge when Fargo caught a graceful movement in the corner of his right eye. He turned to look toward one of the few cabins and paused in midstep, wondering whether his liquor had been drugged.

Two young beauties stood in front of the cabin, one chestnut-haired, the other dark brunette, both dressed and coifed as if to enter Mrs. Astor's parlor. They watched him and Logan with more than passing curiosity.

"This can't be," Fargo said. "I've seen some beautiful soiled doves in fancy feathers, but not in filthy creek camps."

Logan followed Fargo's gaze. The girl with chestnut hair especially drew their attention. Her fancy gown of claret-colored brocade was boldly risqué by current American standards, Santa Fe excepted. The bodice fit snugly around her trim waist and dipped generously at the neckline. What it revealed made Fargo swallow hard.

"She's proud of her tits," Logan said. "I can't really blame her."

The brunette seemed less sensual, at first glance, but beautifully regal. Her hair, shiny black as a raven's wings, was swept up under a wide-brim felt hat with a gay pink ribbon circling the low crown.

"The one with her tits trying to make a jailbreak," Fargo said, veering off toward the two women, "is giving us a smile as big as Texas. Let's go pay our respects and find out what the hell they're doing here."

The two men strolled closer and Fargo touched the brim of his hat. "Ladies, my name—"

"Is Skye Fargo," supplied the chestnut-haired lass in the risqué gown. "And the gentleman with you is Mr. Logan Robinson."

Fargo wished he could swim in those liquid, honey-colored eyes, shimmering pools of feminine vitality—and subtle invitation.

"You have the advantage on us," Logan told her.

"My name is Adrienne Myers," spoke up the more demure brunette, smiling hesitantly, "and the enthusiastic woman who just greeted you is Ursula Langford. We guessed your names because one of the prospectors, a nice man named James West, told us you were coming."

Fargo admired how a fine gold herringbone chain offset eyes the perfect blue of forget-me-nots and accentuated the soft white skin and delicate bones of her throat.

"Adrienne," Ursula volunteered, "reads Shakespeare and Milton, and you should hear her rattle off Chaucer in Old English."

"Middle English," Adrienne quietly corrected her.

"But I," Ursula nattered on, "like shilling shockers and those naughty books from France with the blue covers."

She cast a woebegone glance around her hopeless surroundings. "Not that I've read one lately."

She aimed a sly, flirtatious smile at Fargo and added, "So I make them up in my mind, and I go lots further than the writers do."

Fargo smiled back. "No one can hang you for your thoughts."

"Ursula," Adrienne said with gentle reproof, "there's a strict line between flirting and being fast."

Fargo glanced from one beauty to the other, still not believing what he was seeing—not here, in some of the most dangerous, woman-scarce country in the West.

"May I ask the obvious question?" he said.

Adrienne smiled a bit more warmly. "Why are we here? Well, we shan't be much longer, I trust. Our husbands are leading a rescue party for us as we speak."

"They're business partners in San Francisco now," Ursula explained. "We took the new Overland stagecoach from Omaha to California to join them. For that stage of the trip Adrienne and I were the only passengers. But the driver was a heavy drinker, and there was a horrible rollover beside a river east of here—the driver and the guard both drowned, trapped under the conveyance."

"We were only shaken up," Adrienne added, "but we were marooned in godforsaken country, an area we were told is crawling with hostile Indians. And as if by miracle, Mr. West and Mr. Appling and some of the other prospectors encountered us as they returned from a trading post. Several of them had built these cabins so they can stay the winter and resume prospecting at the first thaw. One of them kindly let us use his cabin until we are rescued."

"You're sure that rescue is under way?"

The sudden look Adrienne gave Fargo puzzled him. It was hard to read, and maybe he'd seen nothing but a wayward reflection in those forget-me-not eyes. But that look seemed almost hopeless, as if she had . . . cried out to him in desperate silence for something she knew was impossible to attain.

"We certainly pray that it is under way," she replied, "and it was confirmed that a party has set out. I wrote a letter and Mr. Appling used something called jackass mail to contact our husbands. The prospectors pay dearly for the service and mail couriers show up here perhaps every two weeks. About five days ago I received a reply from my husband telling me that he and Ursula's husband were leaving San Francisco the next day with an armed escort. It's been perhaps ten days since they left."

"They'll be in a hurry," Fargo said, eyes twinkling. "I know I would be. It might have been faster, though, to work through the army."

"Larry wrote that he tried that. The army told him they can send no patrols into the Black Hills until further notice."

Fargo glanced at Logan. "Yeah, we heard something about that."

"We're all in trouble, aren't we, Mr. Fargo?" Ursula asked, her voice tightening. "That Indian attack last night—it was terrifying. I've heard what Indians do to white—"

"Ursula!" Adrienne cut her off sharply.

"You're both in danger," Fargo said frankly, "but you're *not* anywhere near a hopeless situation, so buck up. Allowing for delivery time on that letter, your rescue party will be here any day—maybe even today."

"Is it true, Mr. Fargo," Ursula said, "that you and Mr. Robinson are here to drive the prospectors out?"

"What did Jim West think about that charge?"

"He called it sheep-dip."

"And sheep-dip it is," Fargo answered. He neatly sidestepped any more awkward questions on the subject by adding: "You ladies sure are easy on the eyes. Do you dress and fix up like this every day?"

"Most days," Ursula replied. "You see, the weight allowed for luggage on a stagecoach is frightfully low. So we brought only our best things, planning to buy less formal clothing in San Francisco. Besides, dressing this way . . ."

"She's going to claim," Adrienne took over, "that it keeps us safer around so many . . . lonely men. But I should think that gown she's wearing right now would provoke risks, not deter them."

"Stuff!" Ursula protested. "And Mr. West kindly saw that we have protection night and day."

"Yeah, a gruff old coot named Dad Bodine," Fargo said, grinning. "I just spotted him beside the cabin, giving me the hoodoo eye and deciding whether or not he should shoot me."

Dad Bodine, one of the last survivors of the famous Taos Trappers, was popular and respected on the frontier and still feared for his fighting prowess despite being long in the tooth. Fargo's trail had crossed Bodine's several times, and he liked the old salt. Dad had the easy calm and confidence of men who are good at handling animals and useful in emergencies.

"Just keep it in your pocket, Fargo!" Dad called over. "These two little cottontails is hitched!"

Red splotches leaped into Adrienne's cheeks. "He's a very loyal and good man," she said, "but rather earthy."

"A man who gets right to his point," Logan said, "is rare. Language was invented to disguise our true thoughts and bewitch the intellect."

Adrienne turned to him, visibly impressed at his erudition and moved by his obvious deterioration. "Oh, are you a philosopher, sir?"

Logan swept off his filthy hat and bowed. "Not a philosopher, madam, so much as a careful observer of humankind."

Fargo shook his head when both women gazed upon Logan as if he had just announced the secret name of God.

"Jesus," Fargo muttered, "it's getting deep."

"Thought provoking," Adrienne whispered, her eyes glistening. "'To bewitch the intellect.'"

"It sounds fancy but I don't get it," Ursula complained.

"Plato and I have to be going," Fargo said, barely keeping a straight face.

They bade the ladies farewell and headed toward the bridge again.

"That line you just spouted," he told Logan, "is too rich for my belly."

"I know, it's pure horseshit. I saw it scrawled on a shithouse wall in Nashville. But I've made women drop their linen when they hear talk like that. You saw Adrienne—she melted. Too bad I can't cash in on it anymore. Those two are surely out of their element."

"Yeah," Fargo agreed. For a moment he recalled that strange message Adrienne seemed to send him with her eyes—like she was begging him without words for something beyond hope.

"I hope they get out all right," Fargo said. "But right now we've got some scouting and searching to do. Your brother and his toad-eaters are holed up in these hills someplace, and they're staying on us close. So let's me and you get on them even closer."

6

Stuart Brennan firmly believed that the mouse who had but one hole was quickly eaten—and likewise for men launching a bold criminal enterprise. So he picked his favorite hole and met with his men in a cave near an 1840s massacre site called Chinaman's Chance. The cave entrance was hidden by a magnificent cataract tumbling down from atop a limestone shelf in an explosion of white foam.

"Dobber," Brennan said, voice raised above the constant noise of the water, "I can understand a man missing his target—most bullets *do* miss, after all. But to report that you killed a man when you in fact did not . . . I hired you because I *thought* you were smarter and more resourceful than you look."

Dobber Ulrick, rabbit-faced, slope-shouldered, one side of his neck swollen with an ugly boil, shook his head stubbornly.

"I hit the son of a bitch in the *head*, Mr. Brennan. I seen the blood squirt and his head snap around, and he dropped like a rock."

"Have you never heard of possum players or stun shots? That's why I always tell you boys to include a finishing shot."

"There were two *legends* on that bluff at Fort Pierre," Jack Stubbs said in a sarcastic twang. "Skye Fargo and Logan Robinson. Ol' Dobber here was scared shitless and hauled his freight first chance he got."

"That part was smart of him," Brennan countered. "Those two are very different types of legendary killers, yes, but each is a top hand at keeping undertakers busy. And it's Fargo we must respect most."

"Now see, I don't think that's the way of it, boss," Jack Stubbs said. "Now Fargo, he's the type that's got use to the

36

yahoos and newspaper scribblers crowding around him like flies on a turd. But that ain't what he got this morning at the French Creek camp. He's a puffed-up deal, and once he sees how dangerous it is in these parts, why—"

Brennan raised a hand to stop him, shaking his head in wonder at cussed human ignorance. Light slanting through the cave entrance revealed hard, flat, gunmetal eyes in a face that impressed those who liked polished, brutal men. He wore a new leather weskit and herringbone trousers. Sharp-roweled spurs of fancy Mexican silver protruded behind his oxblood boots.

"All three of you," he said, "have been stall-fed too long and you've got lazy. Jack, you couldn't be more wrong about Fargo. Once he takes on a job, you've got a bulldog on your ankle. He knows these hills and has defeated their dangers. Fargo constantly expects trouble and he meets it head-on. He doesn't believe in letting his enemies set the rules, and there is no limit to how ruthless he is willing to be to defeat them."

"Yeah, Fargo is a rough one," said Waco Clayburn. "But the way you got things set up here, he'll be like a coyote sniffing a hundred holes and finding no rabbit."

This was only one of several widely dispersed caves they were using, and they constantly moved their stock of Indian burner and weapons.

"You're not listening to me, Waco," Brennan said. "All of you hearken and heed. Dobber failed to stop him at Fort Pierre, and right now Skye Fargo is on our spoor, and eventually he *will* find us, mark me. He'll look for us, and those hawk eyes will find sign even an Apache would miss. He won't let go of this no matter what we do, and the longer he stays alive the closer he gets to skinning all of us. Dobber cost us the element of surprise, but the key is still to strike quickly and decisively."

Brennan had their full attention now. He made a pulpit pause to build things up.

"I *mean* it, boys; this isn't pub lore. He'll fix our flints if we don't play this deal smart. That bastard Fargo means to kill all of us—that's why he and Robinson were sent. And until he succeeds Fargo will work on us like a cactus thorn under a callus."

Waco Clayburn was a burly man with sullen, apathetic

eyes and blunt features deeply pockmarked from a near-fatal bout with smallpox. He stubbornly shook his head.

"I'll give you the threat from Fargo," he said, "but Logan Robinson ain't got enough strength left to lick snot off his upper lip."

A grim smile touched Brennan's lips. None of these men knew that Logan was his brother or about the kill grudge that had brought Logan here.

"Only when he's dead will Logan Robinson cease to be a threat," Brennan assured him. "By the way, Waco—are you feeding the prisoners?"

"Twice a day like you said."

"Good. And keep a close eye on the pack mules."

Brennan pulled the gold-cased watch from his fob pocket and thumbed aside the cover to check the time.

"Jack, have a case of liquor and a crate of Spencers ready to haul to Bear Butte. We're meeting a renegade named Swift Canoe near there right after sunset."

Stubbs nodded.

"We've got a war to stir up, and quick," Brennan added. "Fargo's out there now, and remember to stick to your ambush spots and wait for him—if you move around too much, patrolling for him, you'll never hear the shot when he kills you."

Fargo spent most of his first full day in the Black Hills making his way steadily north and trying to think like his foes.

"A cave would be the best place to hole up around here," he told Logan. "But there's no way in hell we can take the time to search for it. There're likely hundreds in these hills, and besides, that raid last night at French Creek means the trouble's already started."

The two men had stopped to water their mounts from a seep spring just south of Spruce Gulch and a few miles west of Deadwood Creek.

"You're the dealer," Logan said, bracing himself on his saddle horn. "But wouldn't all that mean they'd want an area that was most safe from discovery and convenient for meeting with renegades?"

Fargo nodded. His eyes did not stop prowling the wooded slopes around them.

"Yeah, that shines. They've got liquor, guns and ammunition to haul around, and it's damn hard to portage anything in this terrain with so few trails and just some narrow Indian traces. That tells me they picked a spot as close as they could get to Bear Butte but still in the hills for concealment. My money's on the northeast tip of the Black Hills."

Ever mindful of ambush Fargo pointed his bridle in that direction, wondering how long it would be before Logan slumped dead out of the saddle.

So far he was holding up, but just, and clearly he was at the scrag end of his endurance before the hard part had really begun. And the moist, chilly, fall air this high up was no balm for a consumptive.

Colonel Durant, Fargo told himself, made a mistake in hiring this man. He belonged in a sanitorium, not traipsing all over the *Paha Sapa* and becoming a liability to Fargo. And the more exhausted he got, the more he ran his mouth.

"It's the same old shit over and over," Logan remarked after they had ridden perhaps thirty minutes in silence. "Most of those prospectors at French Creek might not be able to sign their own names. But they're smart enough to know they have to cash in and get out quick."

"Sure," Fargo said, hoping he'd shut up.

"Nobody cares about a piece of empty wilderness," Logan went on, "until somebody grubs gold or silver from it, and suddenly there's room in the puddle for only one big frog. And that big frog usually knows a man who knows a man in Washington City."

"Yeah, but this is a little different," Fargo reminded him, vigilant eyes scanning everything. "Your brother's employer wants to profit from supplying a war, not smelting gold. Now whack the cork and keep your eyes peeled. You talk too damn much."

"Unpucker your asshole," Logan shot back, snappish from exhaustion. "We aren't soldiers."

Fargo pulled rein and locked eyes with the killer. "No, but I'm the dealer, remember?"

"Maybe I'm starting not to like that."

"Maybe that's tough shit." Fargo loosened his Colt in the holster. "Didn't take you long, did it, to show your true colors?"

Logan surrendered with a weak grin. "Maybe I'll kill you later. But right now I need your *famous* trail skills to find my brother."

Both men gigged their horses forward, threading slowly through the spruce and aspen. Fargo remembered to watch the movements of the Ovaro's sensitive ears.

"What's your dicker with your brother?" Fargo said.

"The fact that he's still alive. You know, Fargo—those were two very pretty young women we met this morning."

After a long pause Fargo said impatiently, "Is this going somewhere?"

"I suppose not. Their story is common enough on the frontier, so I can't fault it. But the *way* they told it—each taking turns almost like they were reading it. That struck me as a bit rehearsed, perhaps."

"Maybe so. Do you know anybody out West who isn't telling some lies? Could be they're a couple of grifters who fleece prospectors."

Fargo had spotted plenty of game during this ride: wild ducks and geese and pheasants near water, deer, rabbits and quail in the thickets. Once, they had to stop downwind of a three-hundred-pound black bear while it rolled a log aside to get at the beetles under it. Fargo worried more about the larger and meaner brown bears and silver-tip grizzlies native to these fecund hills.

At one point the Ovaro snorted and tossed his head. Both men drew rein.

"He's caught the man scent," Fargo said.

"Indians?"

Fargo shook his head. "He raises more of a ruckus if it's Indians. I've trained him to hate the smell of bear grease."

Logan cocked an eyebrow. "Bear grease? Why?"

"Rock this one to sleep, mother," Fargo muttered. In a louder voice he replied, "Because the males of most tribes rub it into their hair."

"If he's caught man scent, does that mean these men are close?"

"Nah. This stallion has a good wind nose—they could be miles off. If they were real close, he'd stutter-step, too. But it tells me we might be headed in the right direction."

"Could just be more prospectors he smells."

"Distinct possibility. Deadwood and Whitewood Creek are up ahead, and they're both known for nugget-bearing pockets behind rocks along the bottom. Rest here. I'll be a while."

Fargo lit down and dug his binoculars out of a saddle pocket. He stretched the kinks from his back and then selected a tall ponderosa pine, shinnying up into the lower branches and then climbing as high as he could.

Careful to keep the lenses from reflecting the westering sun, Fargo slowly studied the vista of slopes, forests, sculpted pinnacles and sinewy creeks. Often it wasn't possible to see past the canopy of trees. But Fargo gave them plenty of attention, anyway, alert for the sudden flight of birds.

But it was in a small meadow among the trees where Fargo spotted the rider.

It was a copper-tinted Indian brave, strong and in his prime, but at first Fargo couldn't identify the tribe. At first sighting he usually went by the way the hair looked, each tribe cutting and wearing it differently.

But this brave wore his hair cropped ragged and short. Either he was in mourning, Fargo thought, or he was one of the strange breed of renegades called "contrary warriors" who sometimes came to the Black Hills seeking visions at the sacred lake.

A bit more study told Fargo this was a Cheyenne, not a Lakota. He wore the wolf-skin medicine pouch of the Wolf clan, and the intricate beadwork on his knife sheath was unquestionably the highly prized work of the Cheyenne tribe, unmatched by any Northern Plains tribes in beadwork decorations.

The brave didn't turn at an angle that allowed Fargo to see his face. A few seconds later he disappeared among the trees.

It's one damn thing after another in these hills, Fargo reminded himself. He hoped this brave wasn't a contrary warrior and that he was just passing through. A contrary warrior fought by his own rules and followed no chiefs, not even renegade leaders, and that didn't bode well for two white intruders snooping around.

After about half an hour Fargo climbed back down, brushed the bark and pine needles from his buckskins, and kicked Logan's foot to rouse him. The consumptive struggled to his feet.

"See anything?" he asked, trying to sound like he hadn't been fast asleep.

"A lone Cheyenne. But we're moving deeper into the northeast chunk. C'mon, butt your saddle."

"At once, sergeant-major."

They pushed steadily on in the direction of Bear Butte, Fargo scouring for recent signs of passage. He figured you couldn't haul an appreciable amount of guns, liquor and ammunition around without leaving traces, but so far the Trailsman had spotted nothing that didn't belong to the place.

They skirted a wide swath of mountain slope that had been stripped of trees to provide supports for mining operations farther west. A late-afternoon sun was losing its warmth and casting long, slanted shadows over the denuded slope. Fargo turned away from the dismal sight.

"We'll push on for another hour or so and make a quick cold camp," he decided. "We'll grab a few hours' sleep and slog on."

"Wouldn't sunrise be soon enough to hit leather? Hell, the sun's still up and look how dark these slopes are."

"Rearguard thinking won't get it done," Fargo said. "We can't let up. We have to locate and kill them before they kill us."

"No quarter, no mercy," Logan agreed. "It's a sound anthem, Fargo, but you're up against Stuart Brennan now."

"They're all one to me," Fargo assured him. "Now pipe down."

They covered a few more miles and it was already dark when they dismounted in a little clearing behind a tangled deadfall. They gnawed on beef jerky and shivered when the wind gusted. Between gusts Fargo pulled half of a skinny Mexican cigar from his pocket and fired it up.

"Fargo," Logan remarked after wrapping himself in his blanket, "you've seen the elephant—has anything ever scared you? I mean really shrivel-your-nuts scared you?"

"Hell yes. A Comanche war party, a rampaging grizz, a rockslide or two that damn near turned me into a grease stain. The list goes on."

"What about death—I mean the *idea* of it?" Logan pressed.

"I'm no great shakes at looking too deep into things."

"That might change if you were dying."

"Well, I ain't. Death has to be more or less staring me down before I give it much thought, and even then I only think about how to avoid it, not understand it. Now get some sleep."

As usual Logan ignored him. "Well, I am staring it down and that's when a man goes over his regrets. Sure, even I have a few scabs on my memory. But you know, Fargo, seeing those two beauties earlier reminds me—at least I enjoyed endless female conquests when I was healthy."

"Bully for you. Sleep."

"Women are just a card game—what you drop in one hand you pick up in the next. All you have to do is treat a pretty woman with indifference and she's yours. I recall a schoolteacher—"

"Damn it, Brennan, I ain't here to listen to your deathbed memoirs. All your damn flap-jaw could be drowning out sounds we need to hear to stay alive. You have to put your mind to this job, savvy that?"

It was quiet for a few seconds and Fargo listened to the insect rhythms, the soughing of wind in the trees, the long, rising-and-falling howl of a coyote, ending in a series of sharp, yipping barks. And then Logan ended the peace by suddenly going into a coughing spasm.

"You're a pain in the ass but you're right, Fargo," he said when he recovered his breath. "I know this thing can't be done slapdash, and I know I haven't put my mind to it enough. From here on out I'll do my damnedest to put a tether on my tongue."

"Horseshit. I can tell from your tone that you have no plans to shut up."

"I'll try, but before I do I just want to tell you the one regret I do have: soon I'll die and then I'll never be able to cut the wolf loose again. That's the real pleasure in life, greater even than taking a woman."

"Nothing's better than that," Fargo said bluntly.

"Fargo, I'm not talking about a bust or a tear or shooting at the moon like drunk cow nurses—I mean letting the black beast out."

"And by that you mean murder?"

"Sometimes, yes. I'm just being honest with you in case you should decide to pity me—or trust me."

"No danger of either. Now put a stopper on it and get some shut-eye."

But Fargo wasn't as sleepy as he sounded. Already caught

between white killers and red, and the prospect of brutal gold-camp justice, he also faced this unpredictable murderer whose brain might be deteriorating with his body.

He was weak, exhausted, less and less tolerant of Fargo's bossing—this was a man who killed on impulse, and that "black beast" of his was as close to the surface as a young girl's blush.

Kill him, urged a survival instinct buried deeper than thought, *before he kills you.*

A twig snapped behind Fargo.

And then he heard the wheezing bellow that meant Logan was already asleep. That twig couldn't have been him. . . .

Fargo had the Arkansas toothpick only halfway out of its sheath when an attacker lunged out of the darkness.

7

A cannonball of hard muscle and implacable will slammed into Fargo and drove him back to the ground.

The breath was knocked out of him and he was pinned on his right side, arm trapped and unable to jerk the toothpick. Most fights ended up on the ground, but Fargo was damned if he was going to start out there.

He coiled his muscles like tight springs and exploded them as one, flinging his attacker off. Very little moonlight penetrated the canopy of the forest, and Fargo saw only a sliding shadow. The Trailsman was up in a heartbeat and had just jerked his foot up to tug the knife out when a jarring kick to the crotch sent him off balance.

The attacker was tenacious and dived on Fargo like a snarling wolverine. Unable to recover his feet, Fargo turned his enemy's attack against him, falling back fast in the direction of the dive and making him overshoot Fargo with his excess force.

They came up at exactly the same time and the attacker attempted to put Fargo back on the ground with a sweeping hook of his leg. But Fargo's strong legs withstood the attempt and he threw a short uppercut that didn't land squarely in the dark but backed the attacker up.

It's an Indian, Fargo realized, likely that Cheyenne he saw earlier—his instinct was to wrestle, not fistfight. And the point of that was to sink his razor-sharp, single-edged obsidian knife into Fargo's lights. Fargo had seen no such knife, but fighting for his life against a strong Cheyenne buck in near-total darkness was no time to make safe assumptions.

Again the shadowy form lunged at him before Fargo could get his knife to hand, a so-far successful and deliberate tactic. Fargo managed to apply a rolling hip lock to break the charge.

45

Before his assailant could plant his feet again, Fargo succeeded in flipping him over his back hard with a powerful flying mare.

The brave crashed loudly into the undergrowth, waking up Logan. He fired two quick shots into the air, and Fargo heard the Indian escaping into the trees.

"Stop shooting," Fargo said to the darkness. "I'm pretty sure it was that Cheyenne I saw earlier. He just hightailed it."

"So much for how their bear grease alerts your horse."

"This one hasn't got enough hair for grease. But I'm not sure he came to kill me."

"Rape, you think?" said Logan's sarcastic but cultured voice. "Or maybe he just wanted to meet the hero of *Skye Fargo, Frontier Slayer.*"

Fargo ignored the jabs. "He mighta had a blade in his teeth, but I felt both his hands when we were tussling and there was no knife."

"Look, he meant to kill you, but you were too quick for him, that's all."

"Anyhow," Fargo said, "so much for any sleep right now. We can't stay here now that you've fired your gun. Let's move the horses to a good spot and tether them. We'll get around better in this dark on foot. We're close to a trail that can accommodate pack animals, and it's the best way to head toward Bear Butte."

Fargo's plan, after the two men had set out on foot, was to make his way to the very northeastern point of the Black Hills. It was down on the plains, between Bear Butte and the forested hills, where most illegal dealings with renegades took place. The light would be better down there and Fargo hoped to see and follow the criminal interlopers.

His plan changed in a heartbeat, however, when a bit ring clinked less than fifty feet away.

The sound came from just around the shoulder of a low hill. Fargo put his hand on Logan's shoulder to stop him.

"Come up behind me slow," he whispered. "It's damn dark here, so if it gets to a shooting fandango and I'm out ahead of you, I'll stay low and you aim high to clear me. Put each foot down careful and slow and try to use wind gusts to cover your movement."

Again Fargo heard the clink of a bit ring, the creak of

saddle leather. Moving from tree to boulder to bush Fargo rounded the shoulder of the hill and moved in closer.

Now they were only a fox step away, but still too shadowy to make out clear targets. But Fargo realized those weren't bit rings he heard clinking; it was bottles.

Fargo resisted the temptation to just fan his hammer now. But why try to follow them? This was perhaps a chance to kill Stuart Brennan and his paid thugs, but in this cavernlike darkness Fargo didn't have the firepower without Logan backing his play. Both men had spare cylinders and could manage twenty-four shots between them, and now he regretted leaving the Henry with the horses.

Logan was doing a reasonably good job of advancing quietly behind him, and Fargo waited impatiently. He had pulled his Colt but didn't want to alert Brennan's bunch too early by cocking it.

Logan was drawing near, a shadow taking human form, when Fargo abruptly sensed disaster, the back of his neck tingling.

There was a sudden, slithering noise and Fargo immediately thought of the abundance of timber rattlers high in the Black Hills. For several eternally long seconds menace seemed to mark the very air, and Fargo tried to think of a way out, and then it was too late.

The slithering noise again, a sharp intake of breath followed by a curse from Logan and then a shot from his Navy. That panic shot brought hell down on the two men as repeating weapons began hammering at their locations.

All around Fargo small branches snapped and fell, chips of bark stung him like buckshot, bullets snapped past so close they seemed personal about killing him. He waited for the inevitable lull as they emptied their magazines, and when it didn't come Fargo realized they had multiple weapons ready and loaded.

Logan materialized at his side. "They're giving us muzzle flash. Let's unlimber."

Fargo welcomed his bored, professional tone. He had watched men get rattled under heavy fire like this, start repeating useless actions over and over or just freeze up. Most of those men were dead. But Logan, obviously, was no virgin at a close-quarters lead bath.

"All right," Fargo said. "But we can't burn up all our rounds for one scrape. As soon as you empty both wheels, fade fast back to where we left the horses."

They both cocked and fired at the same time, then split up and moved to a new spot after each shot. It kept up a steady, accurate peppering while also confusing Brennan and his dirt-workers about their location.

Logan showed a bedrock-steady hand and a resolute desire to kill first that matched Fargo's. Fargo heard men cursing and barking orders, and at least one pack mule had caught a bullet—Fargo heard it squealing and had to tighten his lips against the awful sound.

But the stubborn return fire never ceased, and each time he heard that telltale snap Fargo wondered how many more times he could cheat the reaper. His hammer clicked uselessly after his twelfth shot and he took off to the south, rounds chunking in all around him nineteen to the dozen. Logan's gun fell silent seconds after his.

The snake-skittish consumptive had bollixed up the element of surprise. But Fargo didn't rate their ambush a failure. Considering they had only short irons, they gave nearly as good as they got and rattled the criminals. Fargo wanted them nervous, unsure and therefore careless.

But the other elements in this explosive mix—besides a Cheyenne renegade with a mysterious purpose—were the Sioux and the prospectors at French Creek. Again, as he made his way toward the rendezvous point, Fargo thought of Adrienne.

Had she sent him a desperate, pleading look, or had he just been bewitched by the light playing in her eyes? After all, they were the kind of eyes that could show four moods in one minute. He hoped the two women had been rescued by now.

And then again he hoped not. Ursula's inviting eyes like pools of honey lingered in his mind and goaded him to arousal.

He needed to ride back to French Creek anyway. Those prospectors were being goaded to Indian slaughter, or targeted for slaughter themselves, to start a wider regional war between the Dakota Territory tribes and the whiteskins. How they reacted in the next few days was critical.

Fargo knew the gold-fevered, Indian-fevered, trigger-happy element at French Creek might kill him and Logan at the drop of a hat. But with the good will of Jim West and a few others, maybe Fargo could get through to these sourdoughs before they played right into Brennan's greedy, murdering hands.

"Not much time," Fargo muttered, "before it's root hog or die."

It was late afternoon by the time Fargo stepped onto the rope-and-plank bridge crossing French Creek. Prospectors dotted the water in both directions. He saw no sign of the two women.

"At least these hotheads had enough sense to take that dead Sioux off display," Fargo remarked.

"I doubt if *he* cares," Logan replied. "How 'bout a bracer?"

Fargo nodded and they veered toward the saloon tent, almost deserted at this hour. Each man took his turn drinking Taos lightning from a chained-down metal cup. The strong liquor burned in a straight line to Fargo's stomach and made his nostrils sting.

"Shit's awful," Logan sympathized, "but it's got a potent kick if you survive the swallow. Must be the gunpowder."

Jim West stepped into the open-sided tent. He was accompanied by a paunchy, middle-aged man with jaundiced skin like yellowed ivory.

"That fellow's been prospecting too long," Fargo remarked. "Bad diet is about to plant him."

"Saw you come in," West greeted Fargo. "Skye Fargo, Logan Robinson, this is Danny Appling. He's sorta our unelected honcho. He was working his claim last time you was here."

"Mr. Fargo, a pleasure," Appling said, giving Fargo a grip. He ignored the wasted, ashen form of Logan.

"We heard one helluva ruckus echoing from the north last night," West said.

"The direction you two rode in," Appling added. "Sioux?"

Fargo sent Logan a warning glance. The loyalties in this camp, assuming there were any, were likely strongly divided. Admitting they had a shoot-out with white men, at a time when the Lakota Sioux were greasing for war, might not set too well—especially since Fargo couldn't give details about his current job or who those white men were.

"It was pitch-black and hard to tell," he replied evasively, adding: "Were Adrienne and Ursula rescued?"

West shook his head. "I been frettin' that. This ain't no place for fine-haired women. But anything could be delaying that rescue party, 'specially if it's a buncha city greenhorns."

"I'm just curious, Jim," Fargo said. "When you and the others came across the women, did you drag the coach out of the river? Was the team drowned?"

"It was Danny actually found 'em," West replied. "The rest of us took another direction and caught up on the trail from the trading post at Last Chance Bend on the Belle Fourche."

"Wasn't nothing I could do," Appling explained. "The horses and the men was dead, the men pinned underwater by the coach. That was out on the open plain, with Sioux all around and I had two women to rescue."

Fargo glanced at Logan, who nodded slightly as he caught Fargo's drift.

"That makes sense," Fargo said. "But when Adrienne and Ursula told it, I got the impression Jim was with Danny when they were found."

Appling's sunburned face wrinkled like a rubber mask when he frowned. "Nope, it was just me. The current was starting to pull the coach in deeper, and by now I expect it's miles downriver, maybe caught in a snag."

"Likely," Fargo agreed.

It was turning full dark by now and the saloon keeper had lighted several coal-oil lamps suspended on ropes from the tent's overhead supports. Weary prospectors wandered in to drink, smoke, wolf down a greasy rabbit stew and compare the day's gold take with others in bragging tones.

Among them, Fargo noticed, was the choleric-tempered, red-bearded prospector named Clancy, who hugged his Greener like a favorite pet. He took down several quick belts of the potent liquor, never taking his eyes off Logan until it became conspicuous to everyone that he was on the scrap.

"Is there a fly on my nose, Red?" Logan finally asked him, raising his voice with an effort. "Or does this mean matrimony?"

"I ain't got nothin' to say agin Fargo," Clancy replied. "But *you* ain't worth the slime from a maggot's ass, lunger—you back-shooting coward."

"Take it easy," West warned him. "The liquor's got you brain-tangled."

"Whiskey talk is straight talk, by God! That killer ain't here for no good reason, I'm telling yous! Let's jerk him to Jesus *now*!"

"Come down off your hind legs, Clancy," Appling put in. "A careful man tries not to put the noose before the gavel."

"Sell that to the Quakers! This is the Black Hills, you knucklehead, not Fiddlers' Green!"

He laid his scattergun on the counter, and as he spoke one fist beat the palm of his other hand to emphasize his points.

"A *careful* man? Katy Christ! We can't afford to be careful here, and the only circuit judge in these hills is Sam Colt. I got no beef with Fargo, but I sure-god wonder why he's throwed in with a murdering scut like Robinson."

"I said take the pine cone outta your ass," Appling snapped.

By now Clancy was so agitated his Adam's apple bobbed up and down as he spoke.

"I'll take a cat's tail outta my ass! I got months of backbreaking labor to perfect, Danny. Robinson ain't just a killer—he's a thief, and a slick one the law can't nab. He's a bedroll killer if I ever seen one. I say we find a branch and boost him!"

Clancy raised the cup to his mouth, but just as his lips touched it a short iron spoke its piece and the cup leaped from his hand. Gray-white smoke billowed around Logan, and the sulfurous stench of spent powder stained the air.

"I rarely shoot to miss," Logan said quietly. "And since I've never aspired to be an honorable man, I won't require an apology for your various imputations against my character. But you're *fortunate* that I'm a murdering scut—if you'd hurled those insults about Fargo, he'd've put an airshaft through your head by now. You'd best learn to bridle your tongue."

Clancy opened his mouth to retort, and the Colt Navy leaped again. Clancy yelped in pain and cupped his left ear.

"Moses on the mountain!" exclaimed the prospector next to Clancy, pulling the hand away. "That lunger blowed his earlobe clean off!"

This was so diverting that the tent erupted in cheers. But Fargo knew that reaction would change among this mercurial bunch.

"You damn showboater," Fargo muttered, jerking Logan into motion and leading him out of the tent. "Yeah, they're cheering you now, trick shot. You broke up their monotony for a few minutes. But some are already stewing, and there *will* be hell to pay—and we'll be picking up the tab."

8

Nighttime strikes by liquored-up renegades were a constant threat now. The two men first retrieved their mounts and forded the quick-flowing mountain creek. The water came up only to Fargo's thighs, but the sharp, slippery rocks on the bed forced him to lead the Ovaro slowly.

They led their mounts past the common corral and toward the cabin sitting on a rise at the far end of camp.

"You know," Logan said, "nobody around here seems to give a frog's fat ass about that coach and the two men, do they? Even the women—those seem like two very nice gals who should make a bigger deal out of it."

"Yeah, something's crossways there. The thing of it is, nobody saw this rolled-over coach but the women and Dan Appling. Jim West is straight grain clear through and I believe he's telling the truth as he sees it."

"But Appling bristled like a pissed-off lapdog when you asked for details. Still, nothing I've heard is beyond believable. I take it you're starting to wonder if those two visions of heaven are linked to my brother?"

"Aren't you?" Fargo demanded.

"Not seriously, but I commend your caution. I think those women are a couple of high-rolling grifters. It wasn't their plan to come to a rough hole like this. There was no coach rollover—I'd wager they were tossed off at a way station for plying their grift. Maybe Appling did meet up with them. You've seen how homely he is and what lookers they are."

"You're thinking maybe they got him het up with their sex and he's somehow in cahoots with them?"

"Why not? Maybe they even gave him a little taste right

there on the plains. Women that gorgeous could corrupt the pope."

"Easy," Fargo agreed. "But why couldn't your brother be the one who's in cahoots with them?"

"Because neither woman is low enough. I've seen the women he surrounds himself with and they're a coarse, hard lot of painted cats with tongues salted in vinegar. Stuart leaves a smear like a snail, and so do his women."

Fargo rolled the problem around in his mind. "Those gals could be up to something, but we got nothing to prove it. Even if their story isn't quite jake, it doesn't mean they're hardened criminals. They could, like you say, be two very pretty grifters who got marooned near here and now they're planning to milk these clodhoppers for their gold."

"You've seen it plenty before."

Fargo nodded. "It's common as your uncle Bill. And if that is all they're up to, I'm keeping my nose out of the pie. It only matters to me if they're feeding at the same trough as your brother because that puts us in their crosshairs."

"I wouldn't dismiss the possibility," Logan admitted. "But I'd lay odds against it."

They led their horses into a clearing behind the cabin and tethered them.

"Something seems to be agitating the owls in these hills," Logan remarked as they headed toward the plank door of the cabin. "I've been hearing them for the past hour."

"Some are owls," Fargo said, "and some are Sioux warriors. They signal one another with owl hoots."

"You think they're watching this place now?"

"Does okra make your piss stink? They're out there."

"Who goes there?" challenged a gravelly voice from the shadows in front of the cabin.

"Hey-up, Dad!" Fargo called out. "How's your love life?"

"I'm holding my own," Dad Bodine shot back and both men laughed—the bad pun was a longtime greeting ritual between them.

"I smell pig shit. You still got that rat-bastard killer with you, Skye?"

"Yeah, he's the cross I bear."

"Lie down with dogs and you get fleas. You'd best kill him quick or keep him shy of here. At least half this camp wants him deader'n a dried herring, and they ain't none too partial to you, neither, for siding him."

"We won't be here long," Fargo assured the old trapper. "Dad, you've spent time in plenty of gold camps—how bad is it here?"

"Boy, I done some cipherin' in the dirt. They's about twenty gold grubbers here pulling in, say, twenty dollars a day each after they buy supplies and such. Most been here 'bout six months. That means you're lookin' at more'n seventy thousand dollars in this camp. They got along more or less until this latest Indian trouble whipped up. Now the worry and suspicion has drove some of 'em half-crazy."

"I've seen common troubles knit men," Fargo said.

"Me, too, but there's some bad eggs in this bunch. When the fandango comes—and she's a-comin' with a bone in her teeth—it'll be every swinging dick for himself and the devil take the hindmost. Only, it'll be the Sioux taking their hair."

"And that mysterious camp crier a few days back," Fargo said, "has only muddied the water more. These men are already nerve-frazzled and jumpy, and here I come riding in only a day after this good Samaritan tells them I'm here to drive them out or kill them."

"Tell the truth and shame the devil! And draggin' that curly wolf along with you don't win you no jewels in paradise, neither. Jim West and a few others are speaking out for you, Skye, but how in tarnal hell can they paint this lily beside you anything but black?"

"A man's gotta play the hand he's dealt," Fargo said. "These prospectors should worry less about me and Logan and more about the Sioux."

"Brother, they won't buy that if we bottle it. I've told ever' one of 'em: way I kallate it, they're *all* gone beavers happens they don't pull up stakes priddy damn quick. They don't credit my claim about how smart and battle savvy a Sioux warrior is."

"These Indians lately are drunk," Fargo said. "That'll change if the branches of the tribe go into a big war council."

"Skye, these girls got to get out of here. I ain't dustin' my hocks till they do, but a massacre's close, boy, and no two ways about it."

"Dad," Fargo said, "what's your honest size-up of Adrienne and Ursula?"

"I love 'em both. I love 'em so much I'd close my eyes if they was naked and spread-eagle in front of me."

"You're old, all right. Never mind that—do you believe the story they told?"

"Not by a jugful!"

"Why?"

"Who needs a reason? A female is a natural-born liar, and I never believe a word they say. They'll kill you, too, if they get the itch for a new man. But when calicos look and smell as good as these two does? Boy, they can piss down my back and tell me it's raining."

Logan snorted. "Blind justice speaks."

A rifle hammer clicked loudly. The weapon wasn't easy to make out in the dark, but Fargo knew it was Dad's beloved mule-eared Kentucky rifle.

"Easy, Methuselah," Logan said.

"Don't burn him down, Dad," Fargo said as he knocked on the door. "Believe it or not, he's working for the right side this time."

"Ahuh. And the devil can quote Scripture, too, when it suits his purpose."

Adrienne Myers, again lavishly dressed and breathtakingly pretty, greeted both men warmly. The small cabin had been divided precisely in half with horsehair blankets tossed over a taut rope. The half Fargo stepped into was the bare-bones kitchen, a small plank table, a few three-legged stools and a glowing hearth with something that smelled mighty good cooking in a Dutch oven.

"We have only three stools, but both of you must stay for supper," she insisted in a voice soothing as a bubbling stream. "My cooking is improving. All the lumps in the mashed potatoes are the same size now."

Fargo grinned at her quip. "We'd admire to," he said.

Adrienne's tone turned wistful. "Oh, how I long for an indoor convenience and doors with china knobs!"

"I'm sure you've been missing many things," Fargo remarked, his suggestive tone making her flush.

"Is that you, Skye?" came Ursula's voice from behind the blankets. "Come and say hello. I'm decent . . . sadly."

Fargo ducked through an opening at the end of the blanket wall. Ursula sat on the edge of a web bed anchored to the wall. A lone tallow candle cast a burnished glow on her as she worked a horn comb through the long, tangled tresses of her chestnut hair.

Fargo smelled the tang of fresh-scrubbed female skin. He also whiffed the faint lilac odor of her soap—no lye touched *her* pearly skin. She wore a plum-colored serge dress.

"Adrienne and I were told to wear black out West," she greeted him. "It doesn't show the filth. But I don't like funeral colors."

Fargo raked her with his eyes. "Not my favorite, either."

Those pool-of-honey eyes watched him from under long, sleepy lashes. The smile she gave him was restive, as if a secret, naughty thought had just occurred to her.

"Interesting smile," Fargo said. "Mean anything?"

"Perhaps it just means I'm curious."

"My life is an open book," Fargo lied. "Curious about what?"

"Maybe," she said, lowering her voice and setting the comb aside, "I'm just one of those curious women who often wonder how close they can get to the fire without getting burned."

He watched how the waterfall tumble of her hair gleamed like sunlit gems in the candlelight.

"That works out just fine," Fargo assured her, stepping closer, "because I'm wondering if there's any fire behind your smoke."

Fargo sailed his hat onto the bed and swept her up in his arms, kissing her full on the lips, then deeper as her mouth eagerly accepted his and their tongues sparred with the frenzy of pent-up lust.

Her soft contours molded to him in surrender. Fargo had expected a little reluctance in her, something some married women feigned at first, and he was pleasantly surprised by the ardor of her response.

"Does that answer your question?" she teased him when

they finally broke for air. Her breath was hot on his neck, and her hands were moving slowly south of his stomach.

"It answers one, but it raises . . . raises some others. . . ."

"Such as . . . ?"

"It'll keep," Fargo assured her as her right hand was now only an inch away from the iron furrow in his trousers.

"It's been too long for me, Skye," she told him in a throaty, urgent, wanting whisper. "A married woman knows what she's missing, and the torrid memories prey on her. They—"

She lapsed into an impressed silence when she felt Fargo's male endowment.

"Sakes and saints, does it *ever* end?" she whispered, her hand eagerly massaging Fargo's charged staff and sending hot, pulsing waves of pleasure tickles deep into his groin.

Adrienne's disapproving voice drifted over the wall of blankets. "It's too quiet in there, Ursula—remember that you're a married woman."

"We're just flirting," Ursula called back. "Don't be such a prude."

Her busy hand gave Fargo a see-you-later squeeze. She rose on tiptoes.

"There're places to do it around here," she whispered in his ear. "Maybe even tonight."

Fargo was used to quick surrenders from women at every rung in society, even used to some of these women going after it aggressively as Ursula was. But in truth he didn't give a damn what she was up to; he wouldn't get an hour of peaceful sleep until he rode this lass hard and fast.

Fargo stood there waiting for his arousal to subside. But Ursula's wanton lust had triggered his own and his manhood refused to cooperate. He grabbed his hat and was forced to cover his crotch with it when he stepped into the kitchen. Adrienne didn't fall for his ruse and blushed deep.

Logan, slumped on one of the stools, snickered, then tried to look innocent.

"It's not funny," Adrienne snapped. "Mere flirting doesn't make a man resort to *that*."

"Beg pardon," said an embarrassed Fargo, on the verge of coldcocking Logan.

Fargo waited until he was girded with a hot meal of venison, seasoned with pepper and wild onions, baked potatoes and plum pudding, all eaten standing up. Adrienne poured out glasses of applejack afterward.

Believing Logan to be a college man, Adrienne looked at him solemnly. " 'Know'st thou yesterday, its aim and reason? Work'st thou well today for worthier things?' That's Goethe—do you recognize it, Mr. Robinson?"

"Worthy things are not my specialty, Mrs. Myers, although I have heard of the gent."

"Oh, he's wonderful! Reading him leaves me so . . . so 'inebriate of the senses.'"

"Drunk?" Fargo guessed.

"In a manner of speaking, yes."

Ursula smiled widely at Fargo. "Isn't *she* the prima ballerina? Indians threatening to scalp us at any time, and she's quoting from books."

Surprise, mystify and confuse, Fargo reminded himself. This was a perfect and unexpected moment.

"Ladies," he said cordially, "is there anything you'd like to tell me? Something you're holding back? F'r instance, something that might explain why this rescue party is taking so long?"

Adrienne sent him a quelling stare. "In other words, are we lying to you?"

"I don't go that far," Fargo said. "And I see you're angry at me now."

She pouted prettily for a few moments before a smile formed on those ripe-berry lips. "Let's call it more than a quibble, less than a quarrel."

But again, for just a moment before she had gathered herself after his question, he thought he had seen a silent pleading in those fetching eyes.

"Is Ursula right about the Indians?" she asked. "Are we—"

"Skye!" Dad's bullfrog voice called out. "C'mon out here a minute, wouldja?"

"Renegades?" Fargo asked after he closed the door behind him.

"Not on us yet, but the signs're there. When the wind sets just right, you can hear their drunken caterwauling out on the plains."

"They lost a warrior here," Fargo said. "That's bad medicine for them unless they avenge him. What was done with the body?"

"A few of the men hauled it downstream a fair piece and tossed it into the brush. Nobody would touch his pecker and nuts, so they was left shoved into his mouth. Happens the Sioux find that-ere corpse . . ."

"Carrion might take care of it," Fargo said.

Faint popping sounds from far off reached them on the chilly night wind.

"Gettin' all worked up on coffin varnish and playin' with their new thunder sticks," Dad Bodine remarked. "Sounds like more than in that bunch that attacked last time. Skye, they was crazier'n dogs in the hot moons. Happens they get crazy-brave enough, they can take this camp—and you know what that means for Adrienne and Ursula."

"If an Indian attack turns against you," Fargo reminded him, "you kill the women before they fall into enemy hands. You know that."

Fargo paused as more distance-muffled gunshots reached his ears.

"I make them southeast of here but not yet into the grassland," Fargo said. "How 'bout you?"

"Same."

Fargo headed toward his horse.

"You're smart to go out there alone," Dad called behind his back. "But keep your nose in the wind, boy! I heard the deathwatch beetles tickin' today, and that means somebody's 'bout to die."

9

Following a long-established Indian trace he had known about for years, Fargo bore due east to clear the thickly forested Black Hills. Down on the open plain "directions" became impossible after dark without celestial guidance. Fargo used Ursa Major, the Great Bear, to locate the North Star and get his bearings from the two fixed points.

Constantly orienting with the stars, Fargo reckoned a southeast course toward the vast grassland that began about twenty miles distant. Despite his distaste for fast nighttime riding, he pushed the Ovaro hard knowing that right now time was his worst enemy.

Fargo intended to stall any attack on the French Creek camp and then return to his paid job: killing Stuart Brennan and his literal war machine. Fargo would likely have left those fool prospectors to their own ill-chosen fate and the machinations of the pus-guts in the Indian Ring.

But the unexpected presence of those two women forced him to uphold an unwritten code that he tried to honor when he could.

For Fargo it didn't matter that, if drunk, the Sioux would be far less effective in their attacks. The prospectors had already killed one, and it was not the Lakota way to treat the death of their own lightly—especially when a warrior had died without singing his death song that allowed him into the Land Beyond the Sun.

One was trouble enough, all right, but if those defenders at French Creek killed enough of them, even renegades, the entire Sioux and Cheyenne nations could strike the warpath. And since Fargo was in no position to move those women somewhere safe, his only immediate option was this dicey nighttime ride.

Besides, there was always the chance of crossing paths with Brennan's bunch.

Before long Fargo switched from star reckoning to his ears as the sounds of drunken revelry reached him more clearly. Gunshots, war yips and eventually the individual shouts that sounded like braves firing up their fellow warriors with war talk—all these guided Fargo toward the Sioux renegades. A yellow-orange glow ahead marked their buffalo-chip fires.

He topped a low rise and pulled rein, immediately dismounting to lower his skyline. Fargo could see some of the renegades closest to the fire now, a sight that made him mindful of the nearness of death and momentarily grateful these fearsome warriors were drunk.

They wore bead-adorned buckskin shirts and leggings, and many had scalps dangling from their sashes. They had not painted in the traditional Lakota war colors. Instead, their faces were starkly streaked with charcoal—black symbolizing joy at the death of an enemy.

Some of the braves were so incapacitated by the strychnine-laced strong water that they were almost walking on their knees. Fargo watched one pull a burning chip from the fire and set his own hair on fire, others egging him on by firing their new thunder sticks recklessly. Fargo spotted at least one brave sprawled facedown and wasn't sure whether he was dead drunk or just dead.

The sight disgusted Fargo and reminded him: despite the good intentions of the Quakers and some others, there could be no real meeting of the white and red minds. Their beliefs could never mesh. Fargo knew the free-ranging Indians had no intention of being forced to grow gardens and answer roll calls as many of the conquered tribes now did. And even though Fargo had packed Indian heaven with a fair amount of souls, on that point his stick floated with theirs.

He backed the nervous and lathered Ovaro down the rise a few yards and hobbled him, leaving the Henry in its saddle scabbard. Then Fargo flattened himself at the top of the rise for a better look.

Hawk eyes honed by years of intense observation studied the faces below. After a few minutes Fargo recognized the renegade leader, Swift Canoe of the Hunkpapa Sioux. He was a fierce warrior with a heavy coup stick, but he had rebelled at council and left the tribe with a dozen or so young followers.

Fargo couldn't get an accurate count of them. Many drifted in and out of the circle of firelight, and the shadowy dark beyond it seemed to shimmer with shape-changing shadows as Swift Canoe's followers moved around.

It was the quickly erected rope corral that most interested Fargo. He couldn't spot a guard in the darkness. The half-wild Indian scrubs appeared to be tightly bunched and not exactly liking it.

They're keyed up, Fargo thought. His abdomen tightened at the idea of sneaking up on horses trained to hate the whiteman smell—sometimes even trained to savagely attack them.

He figured he'd have a chance if he stayed downwind, but out here on the open plain winds shifted directions in a heartbeat.

Fargo didn't need to speculate about what would happen to him if he were captured messing with their highly prized mustangs—the equivalent of the white man's high-denomination currency. He had witnessed Sioux wrath firsthand and been grateful he had a strong stomach.

Fargo moved out in a low crouch, quickly at first and often jutting one way or the other: it was sustained motion in one direction that often caught the eye.

For the moment the brisk wind was in his face. Fargo strained his eyes as he advanced, trying to spot a herd guard.

Celebratory gunshots and coyote yips still raised a din. Fargo heard a brave off to one side retching in the darkness. Now Fargo was only about fifteen yards from one of the horsehair ropes holding the mustangs.

Still he didn't spot a guard, and that bothered him. Better to know where they were than to assume they weren't there.

Fargo debated: he could cover this last stretch at a slithering crawl or dash forward, cut the rope, and run like hell. Either option had its drawbacks.

But Fargo's biggest problem was that several of the more cautious and experienced braves had their favorite war horse with them, connected to their wrists by ropes on the head-stalls. The Ovaro had just made a hard run and, despite his speed and stamina, might not have the bottom left to outrun fresh Sioux war horses with their nostrils sliced to increase wind.

Fargo made up his mind and pulled the toothpick from its boot sheath. He dashed forward, sliced the single rope, and pivoted on his heel to escape. As he ran Fargo veered hard to one side to clear the path—his sudden presence alone had spooked the mustangs and they poured out behind him in a chaos of panicked neighing.

Except for one enraged, wild-eyed stallion that shot at Fargo like an arrow from a bow.

Fargo didn't even know it until the screaming stallion, clearly a kill-fighter like his Indian master, was almost breathing on his neck.

Fargo cut hard left, shaking the enraged mustang moment-arily. But it adjusted deftly and was on him again.

He cut hard right, but this time traction gave out and Fargo skidded hard, hitting the ground and rolling from momentum. He stopped on his back and before he could even breathe the moon was blocked out when the stallion reared up to kill Fargo with its dangerously sharp front hoofs.

Fargo had the reflexes of a civet cat and rolled clear by a fractional second. There was no choice—this horse was bent on killing him. He shot to his feet while the mustang was still recovering and vaulted onto its back.

Fargo still clutched his razor-sharp knife. Moving quicker than thought, he hooked his left arm around the stallion's neck and jerked back hard as he sliced into the throat deep with the Arkansas toothpick. Fargo jumped clear of the toppling mus-tang even as it emitted an eerie, fluttery sound like a trumpet when the air was forced out of its collapsing lungs.

The Trailsman bolted for the crest of the low rise with his elbows and knees pumping hard. At first the renegades, drunk and confused, were slow to respond. Fargo knocked the Ova-ro's hobbles off and leaped up onto the hurricane deck, rein-ing the stallion around and thumping him hard with his heels.

"Hee-*yah*!"

The Ovaro flattened his ears and bound forward. By now

the persistent cloud cover had blown over, and a full moon and endless peppering of stars cast a dim, bluish-white glow. Fargo knew he was visible against the sky. When the repeating rifles opened up behind him, a hard chase was on from the braves who had kept their best horses literally to hand.

Fargo felt the reckless, heady surge of brain blood that warned him it was time for immediate action or his life was forfeit.

"To hell with a chase," he decided as he drew back hard on the reins. In for a penny, he told himself, in for a pound.

Fargo tossed the reins forward and swung down out of the saddle, plucking the Henry from its scabbard and levering a round out of the long tube magazine into the chamber.

He dropped into a prone position among a cluster of small boulders and laid a bead on the lead mustang. Fargo hated like hell to kill horses, but one was already dead and it might be the best choice anyway. Most plains warriors highly valued their mounts, but proudly accepted their death in battle because it spoke well for the rider's courage and might even merit a coup feather.

On the other hand, killing Sioux—even hell-bent renegades—in the heart of their ranges would be like trying to smother a fire with gunpowder.

Fargo held his bead, lost it, found it again and wasn't sure he could hold it. The butt of the Henry kicked against his shoulder and the lead horse dropped; the Henry kicked again and a second horse went down, leaving only one pursuer.

Drunk or not, the lone Sioux had good warrior instincts. The mustang began to ride in an evasive pattern, veering suddenly and often and forcing Fargo to scatter-shoot.

The renegade was firing in the direction of Fargo's muzzle flash, and Fargo recognized the distinctive, metallic cracking sound of a Spencer carbine, the seven-shot weapon now carried by some in the U.S. Army.

Fargo rolled to a new position and opened fire. The Henry's lightly oiled mechanisms snicked flawlessly as brass casings shot out the ejector port and rattled against the rocks. The sound of both rifles echoed out across the open terrain in a series of rapidly diminishing *chuff* sounds.

Most of the Sioux's bullets ranged wide of Fargo or fell

well short. One, however, possibly a ground ricochet, grazed the tip of his left elbow and numbed his entire arm for half a minute.

About ten rounds into his magazine Fargo dropped the remaining horse with a fatal hit. It crashed to the ground hard and sent its rider bouncing along like a sack of rags. In seconds Fargo was horsed and pounding his saddle toward the looming mass of the Black Hills.

There was no reason for the renegades to connect this Indian-style ambush with the palefaces grubbing for the glittering yellow rocks at French Creek. Pawnees, Utes and Crows among other tribes were known to ambush and harass the Sioux. Prospectors, on the other hand, rarely fought except on or near their claims.

Fargo only hoped he had impeded the renegades enough to buy a little time.

He had just opened the Ovaro out to a steady lope when something in the corner of Fargo's right eye alerted him.

His head swiveled a quarter turn and he spotted a lone, mounted figure silhouetted on a distant spine of rock, a motionless statue watching Fargo.

The loud whisper made Fargo flinch.

"Don't shoot me, Skye. I've waited here for over an hour and I'm so chilled my teeth are chattering."

Ursula stepped into a rare shaft of silver-white moonlight, tightly wrapped in a blanket.

"You beautiful little fool," Fargo greeted her. "Adrienne and the others must know you're out here."

"I don't care if you don't. Adrienne already knows I'm an adulterer, and besides, she's had at least one lover since our husbands went west."

"Is Dad Bodine out here?"

"He sleeps in the kitchen on a pallet. We made one up for Logan, too. Nobody knew where you went, Skye. Logan said you sneak away every night to engage in unnatural acts with livestock."

She stepped closer, stopping only inches away. Fargo smelled her perfume.

"Where did you go?" she asked him.

"Who cares? I'm back now," he reminded her, brushing a strand of hair away from her eyes.

This time she pressed tightly against him. "I don't know what unnatural acts Logan means. But you can do some with me if you want."

Ursula guided one of his hands under the blanket. Fargo swallowed audibly when a hard, hefty tit filled it, the nipple soft as chamois until he teased it stiff as a bullet.

What she was about to say was so intimate and naughty she rose up on tiptoe and whispered softly in his ear, her breath hot and tickling.

"Skye? Ever since I felt your hard, huge peeder, I haven't been able to quite get my breath. Oh, I want it so much, it feels like wax is melting between my legs! Skye, I want that huge club deep inside me, pounding me until hell won't have it again! Do me right here, please? Do me hard, Skye, and show me what a man is!"

"You're gonna get it good, you hot little firecracker," Fargo promised, his voice husky with a sudden welling of pent-up lust. The almost painful hardness of his arousal was a reminder that it had been too long since the last woman.

She slid the blanket off, revealing a perfectly sculpted body that gleamed like marble in the moonlight, and spread it on the ground while Fargo dropped his gun belt and grounded the Henry.

Ursula lay on her back and bent her legs at the knees as she spread her thighs wide for Fargo. He knelt and dropped his buckskins halfway, Ursula eagerly grabbing his man gland and squeezing it hard.

"My God, Skye, it throbs like it's alive!"

She was so fired up by now that she was panting like a dog in August. She goaded Fargo on by stroking him a few times as she unleashed a whispering torrent of dirty talk, all the time scootching her butt for the perfect entry when Fargo thrust into her.

"Skye! Oh, you're opening me up so wide!" she gasped, hips starting to buck in a rapid rhythm with his. "And going in so *deep*!"

At the moment Fargo didn't give a damn how much she liked it. He was primed to explode, and took her with a savage, plunging force and abandon worthy of the horniest stallion. He lost track of time, place or thought, surrendering to pure, primitive lust, only vaguely aware of the nails clawing deeper into his back, the hoarse whisper begging, demanding, *harder, faster, deeper, Skye. Go deeper!*

About five seconds before his shuddering release the building pressure was so intense Fargo began to twitch violently, out of control from pleasure overload just as Ursula was. Fargo exploded into oblivion like a tight spring uncoiling again and again, and only the cold air on his bare ass finally brought him around, uncounted minutes later.

Or was it, Fargo's mind wondered as the cobwebs of exhausted lust cleared, the ominous click of a hammer being cocked only a foot or so from his head?

10

Ursula, who appeared to have passed out from her erotic exertions, lay naked and still under Fargo, nipples probing and tickling his chest hairs each time she inhaled.

Fargo waited in the chilly darkness, unsure whether he had heard anything.

Dead leaves crunched as somebody moved behind him.

"Now I know when to kill you, Fargo—during the glory of the rut."

"Pull the trigger or leather that lead-chucker," Fargo replied. "My ass is freezing."

"It's leathered, Lothario." Logan Brennan succumbed to a coughing fit.

Ursula stirred under Fargo but didn't quite wake up even though she was shivering.

"You jackass," Fargo told Logan, rising and pulling up his trousers. "I s'pose you watched the whole thing?"

"Didn't see any of it although I heard both of you go into one mighty strong finish. Sounded like a murder scene. I came out here to see if you were back yet. You see, I don't cotton to the idea of you sneaking off and killing my brother before I can."

"Only a few Indian scrubs died tonight when I scattered the renegades' broomtails. I suggest you turn in. We're pulling out early and there's a long day ahead of us."

"When do we quit playing Daniel Boone in the woods," Logan challenged, "and get Stuart and his unsavory associates into a cartridge session?"

"We just had one with them—my Colt's still warm from it," Fargo reminded him.

"Hell, that was shooting at mules in the dark. Just remember, we're paid assassins. That's why your old pal Colonel Durant hired us, right? Not to sugar-tit these females—even if you are getting some good poon out of it."

"You been chewing peyote? Durant also hired us to stave off a war in Dakota. We don't have your brother yet, and by your lights he's hard to lasso. If we do nothing he could spark a war before we kill him. Now get back to your blanket—Ursula's waking up."

"Ursula! I'll be damned. . . . I thought it was Adrienne."

"With those two a man wins a good pot either way," Fargo said. "I told you to leave before she wakes up."

"You'll trim both of them. My favorite is Adrienne. I admire a wily cock tease, and I think that's what she is. Don't shoot; I'm going."

Logan returned to the cabin. That one's trouble, Fargo reminded himself. The way Logan had gotten the drop on him a few minutes ago—that was a deliberate, goading reminder of his talk about killing Fargo any time the impulse moved him.

He's pushing me, Fargo realized. Maybe he was the kind who liked to taunt a man before he murdered him. Fargo still expected him to keel over at any moment from his disease, but if the killer kept pushing, consumptive or not, Fargo would turn it into a call-down or even snap-shot homicide.

When Ursula was awake, Fargo sent her inside first and then waited about fifteen minutes, listening to the night and smoking while he ran everything through his mind. Logan was right: the nighttime ambush against Brennan likely accomplished little. Logan's assassin's instincts told him to move fast and get the job done. But this wasn't like killing a banker in his bed, Fargo thought.

This deal was like a jumble of unstable boulders on a slope—move the wrong one and they'd all go tumbling down, perhaps even crush him. Stuart Brennan and his murdering thugs; renegade warriors with repeating rifles; suspicious, hair-trigger prospectors on the verge of gold-induced insanity; two lovely females with possibly lethal intent; even a skulking contrary warrior whose medicine bundle was the wolf, perhaps out for the trophy of Skye Fargo's hair.

And top all of it off, Fargo mused, with a homicidal sidekick who had the conscience of a pit viper.

"Pile on the agony," Fargo muttered, watching his breath ghost in the cold air.

What was it Dad Bodine had said earlier? *I heard the deathwatch beetles tickin' today, and that means somebody's 'bout to die.*

The night wind gusted, the sound mournful and despondent, and Fargo went inside for a few hours of sleep.

"This Swift Canoe," Logan said while they spelled their horses, "is he a traitor to his tribe or does he just plan to be the heap big chief?"

"You'll see pigs fly before you read a featherhead's thinking. Swift Canoe has always been trouble for his people, but he's not a white man's dog when he stays sober. Brennan has got him and the others tangle-brained from Indian burner, and if Swift Canoe turns on him there goes his joy juice and the repeating rifles."

"They already have the rifles, don't they?"

"Sure, but they're worthless without the bullets, and bullets are hard to come by for an Indian if somebody kills his only suppliers."

"Somebody?" Logan repeated. "You're not the coy type, Fargo. You're afraid to say 'we' because you don't want to admit you were stupid enough to get sucked into this deal. Who can blame you?"

"Thanks for your blessing," Fargo said absently, more interested in their surroundings than in Logan's constant commentary on things.

Fargo judged it was around ten a.m. by the slant of the shadows. They had reined in where a spring of cold, sweet water frothed from a clutch of rocks.

"You know," Logan remarked, "I get the distinct impression you're enjoying the danger—and the prospect of killing."

"Danger adds a little savor to life," Fargo allowed as he inspected his tack. "Also keeps a man sharp and feeds the flies. As for actually enjoying it . . . you ain't exactly a circus."

Logan started to laugh but succumbed to a fit of coughing. Fargo had no idea how this wasted shell of a man was still functioning, but that hacking cough announced their presence everywhere and Fargo was damn tired of it.

Lost in the folds of his dirty corduroy coat, Logan produced his silver flask and shook it. "Damn the luck, I've got out of medicine."

He blew a few lazy smoke rings until a sudden, forceful cough scattered them.

"That cough of yours," Fargo said, "could become our epitaph. You got any real medicine for it?"

"I've been to several doctors—might's well have been African witch doctors. They all told me to drink quinine and boiled sassafras. I tried it and had the drizzling shits for a week. And that damn quinine makes your head ring like you've been mule-kicked. Two of the sawbones told me to get down to the salubrious air of New Mexico."

"So why didn't you? Some people get better there."

"Two territorial warrants, that's why. But I do hope to get back to Fort Pierre before I take the Big Jump."

"So you can ride up on the bluffs and stare at the fort?"

"Maybe. Maybe it just seems like a good place to die."

Fargo let it go and stepped up and over. "Well, you ain't dead yet, so stir your stumps, coffee cooler. You might have to earn your pay today."

The two men had ridden back to the site of their first clash with Brennan. Fargo had examined several recent tracks, comparing the moisture inside them. That and the bend of the grass told him how frequently Brennan used this route and which set of tracks was the most recent—one set made not much longer than twelve hours ago.

Following the track was easy enough, Fargo figured, but not necessarily a wise survival tactic. A smart adversary, knowing of his tracking skills, might set up ambush nests along his own deliberately clear trail. But Fargo was willing to take the right risks because he was determined to keep the pressure on Brennan.

So far he had tossed lead at them in an ambush, stopped one likely Indian attack they provoked, and escaped assassination at Fort Pierre. However, events in the Black Hills were approaching a full boil, and Fargo knew he had to take control quickly or let the odds kill him.

11

Dobber Ulrick thought he spotted motion below.

He snapped out of his waking doze and pushed to his feet, squinting hard and studying the slopes just to the east. Dobber, the deadliest rifle shot among Stuart Brennan's men, had been assigned this ambush nest by the boss himself—a saddle between two tall hills, heavily wooded on its forward slope, rock-strewn on its steeper rear slope.

Motion . . . and color, Ulrick told himself. A flash of black in a very narrow opening along the pack trail below.

Let it be that cockchafer Fargo . . . Ulrick's rabbit face actually managed to look dangerous as seething hatred firmed his features. This might literally be his best shot at redeeming himself for his failure back at Fort Pierre.

If only, he berated himself again, you hadn't jumped the damn gun and swore Fargo was dead. Jack and Waco had taken to mocking him with names like Dead Shot Dobber and Little Miss Completely, the fucking knotheads.

But triumphantly handing Brennan two famous, severed heads just might bring that roweling to a screeching whoa, Dobber figured, grinning at the prospect.

He eased back down onto his knees. Eyes constantly alert now he dug a chunk of salt junk out of the fiber sack dangling from his belt and contentedly gnawed on the cured meat, chewing with his mouth open and making noises that could incite a normal man to shoot him. Now and then spitty clots of meat spewed from his mouth and plopped onto the boulder behind which he knelt. Absently he poked them back into his mouth.

Watching this terrain, Dobber thought, was a bitch. Sure, this was a good nest high up, but the trees formed a dark screen with only occasional openings, and the pack trail itself was too narrow to spot. At the base of this sloping saddle, however, was a twenty-foot gap in the trees beside the trail.

Dobber figured he'd get off two good shots with his Spencer carbine, maybe a third.

Black, he reminded himself. He'd seen the color black in motion.

The exact color of Logan Robinson's coal black Arabian horse . . .

"I've always heard," Logan remarked, "that Indians and Mexicans are the best trackers—far better than most white men."

"I'd say you've heard right," Fargo said. "Now shut up."

"I told you I don't appreciate that tone, Fargo."

"Tough tit. There's a mort of things I don't appreciate about you, Brennan, so pull up your skirts and forget your little peeves. This is a job—that's all."

Fargo, hanging low in the saddle now and then to inspect the tracks, didn't like the way this deal was playing out. Logan insisted his brother was too careful to simply lay down a track to his hideout.

Brennan's first plan, Fargo decided, was another rifle ambush just like the one beside the Missouri just over a week ago.

He hauled back on the reins and then tossed them forward. He swung down and pointed left of the pack trail. Some of the ponderosa and aspen trees had been forced to steep angles like a "V" by a granite shelf crowding through them. It protruded a few feet beyond the trees.

"Can't see much from the trail," Fargo said. "I want to get the lay of our surroundings. I've been through here before, but I can't sight the landmarks."

Fargo took off his hat and edged out onto the shelf until he could see past the trees without showing himself. Despite being a verdant oasis on the dry plains, the domelike Black Hills uplift had plenty of weatherworn places that easily yielded their secrets to experienced eyes. The section out ahead showed where long centuries of erosion had laid bare subsurface areas. Fargo stared at an impressive cliff, its tilting, fully exposed strata overlooking Deadwood Creek like a giant altar.

"Again with the Daniel Boone hokum," Logan spoke up

behind him in an impatient, superior tone. "Let's get some lives over, Fargo."

"Chuck all the chin music," Fargo snapped as he returned to his stallion. "We could be jumped anywhere, and don't be too surprised if the man who cuts your liver out was born with a sunburn. Watch and listen."

"To hell with caution. I don't have that much time to spare."

"It's none of my funeral," Fargo said bluntly, forking leather and gigging the Ovaro forward. "I told you before this isn't a vengeance raid. And if and when you die affects nothing. I *am* working fast, but unlike you I also want to stay alive."

"Don't we all?" Logan said in a sly tone, refusing to meet Fargo's cold stare.

"There!" a jubilant Dobber Ulrick exclaimed. "*That's* medicine!"

Damn it, man, that time he definitely saw it, bold as a big man's ass: a flash of black between two trees. It was the lunger's horse, all right, and that meant Fargo was coming, too.

They were following the pack trail, and before long they would pass through the break in the trees straight below his position.

His Spencer, with its magazine in the butt, wasn't reliable at distances beyond three hundred yards, but Dobber estimated this shot at no more than two hundred. And with luck he'd get off several rounds with the new breech-loading repeating rifle. He'd already timed himself and knew he could fire it accurately seven times in ten seconds, an astounding capability.

He brought the carbine to half cock and made sure there was a cartridge in the chamber.

Two famous men, he reminded himself. One a hero, one a villain, both worth a fortune if they were carved up into souvenirs. Dobber was present when a necklace made from the teeth of Joaquin Murrieta, the "Mexican Robin Hood," sold for five hundred dollars in gold shiners.

"Yeah, c'mon, big hero," he urged Fargo in a whisper. "*You're* the boy I want to pop over."

He laid the barrel of the Spencer atop the boulder and brought the sights in line with the opening below, practicing.

Fargo saw the break in the tree cover coming up on their left and reined in.

Logan remained half-slumped in his saddle while Fargo went forward on foot and cautiously darkened his face with soil to cut reflection before he peered out from the trees.

"More Daniel Boone shit," Logan said in a weary voice. "When are you going to skin a bear?"

Fargo ignored him. On the left as he gazed out was a stretch of the Black Hills sliced by red-washed gullies. But straight ahead and above, a saddle linked two hills. Most of the slope leading up to it was wooded but the saddle was clearly visible above the trees.

"We'd better cut wide to the right here and stay in the trees," Fargo said. "There's a boulder up there where a shooter could notch us plumb center."

"The trees are too damn thick once we leave the trail," Logan complained. "And too damn many low-hanging branches—let's just get up a head of steam and bust through. We're supposed to be relentless predators, right?"

"Who died and left you in charge? Light down and follow me," Fargo said as he followed the granite bench back toward the trail.

"Yeah, I see it now, Fargo. You *don't* want to face down Stuart Brennan and his crew. So you're finding every damn excuse you can dredge up to avoid it. We have to spare the horses, we have to scout, we have to trail, all your other precautions . . . so maybe you're not the rootin'-tootin', hell-bent-for-leather, man-eating son of a bitch you're cracked up to be?"

Logan still sat his saddle, exhaustion making him snarly and defiant. Fargo was about to retort when suddenly it felt like an invisible feather was tickling the bumps of his spine.

Seconds later the insects fell silent.

"Dismount!" he snapped at Logan. "Get off that horse *now*!"

A sudden rustling in the underbrush before a fat, frightened rabbit shot under Logan's horse and across the trail.

The barb spooked instantly and surged forward, Logan taken by surprise and flopping backward over the cantle like a rag doll. The panicked horse bolted into the clear and a rifle spoke its piece. A sound of flat impact and Logan twisted quick to the right, grunting hard on a sharp intake of breath before rolling out of the saddle.

12

Logan landed in sticker bushes where at least he was well hidden.

"Stay where you are!" Fargo shouted, unsure whether he was dead or alive.

He levered a round into the Henry's breech and peppered the saddle in quick groups of three shots. He reserved some of these for chipping at the boulder, keeping it hot up there for anybody still lurking. But no shots were returned and Fargo had a hunch the bushwhacker was making his escape down the back side of the saddle.

Fargo had good tree cover if he decided to head up there. And he figured he had to if he hoped to control these men, not just react to them. He had no idea how bad off Logan was, but Fargo had scouted this area before and he recalled that the back side of that saddle was steep and rock-strewn.

It should take a man fleeing down that slope considerable time to reach his horse.

"How bad you hit?" Fargo shouted over.

"Left thigh. Hurts like hell."

"Yeah, bullets generally do. Heavy bleeding?"

"Just a steady trickle," Logan called back. "I've got my hand pressed on it."

"All right. I'll tend to it when I get back—or maybe that fool Daniel Boone will find you."

"No need to rub it in."

The trees and brush were thick up that slope, and Fargo opted to leave the Henry behind for a quicker ascent. He advanced rapidly, moving from tree to tree, and when he reached the saddle he charged it.

The sandy surface was empty and sand was still sifting into

76

the boot prints made by the man who just fled. Fargo moved through to the other side and was just in time to watch a slope-shouldered man below bend to remove his claybank's hobbles.

Fargo wanted to kick himself in the ass for leaving his long gun behind. This slope wasn't as long as the other one, but there were at least a hundred yards separating the two men—a good fifty or so yards beyond Fargo's aiming range with a handgun.

A steely determination filled him like a bucket under a tap. He *had* to send in his card in a splashy way, and that meant, come hell or high water, killing this cockroach below him.

Fargo searched the sandy, rock-cluttered slope until he spotted a flat piece of shale about ten feet below him. Driven by sheer will to prevail, without the slightest notion in hell whether his next move would be his last, Fargo drew blue steel and charged the piece of shale.

He leaped, landed on it with both feet deliberately skidding, and sent it sliding, Fargo riding it precariously and doing a desperate balancing act to stay upright. It launched slowly but rapidly picked up speed.

Ten yards closer and the shooter stood up, taking up the reins.

Twenty yards closer, Fargo wobbling wildly, and the escaping thug turned a stirrup to mount.

Thirty yards closer, Fargo picking up a gut-tickling speed, starting a small rockslide before him, and the startled man below went slack-jawed when he spotted the bearded avenger rocketing toward him like a genie on a magic carpet.

Forty yards closer, Fargo faster than the wind, and the paid killer had his Spencer in his shoulder socket. Fargo cursed, not only because he was still out of reliable handgun range but because he felt himself losing his balance.

Fifty yards closer, with the Spencer already barking at him, Fargo tilted precariously and opened fire.

Sixty yards closer, both men trading shots in a markedly uneven contest, a stationary rifle versus a man flailing to stay vertical while firing a short gun.

Seventy yards closer, a desperate Fargo down to his last bullet when the shale he was using as a sled shattered and vaulted him into the air like a man diving into a lake. A bullet from the Spencer nicked the toe of his boot, and in a final effort, still airborne, Fargo forced a bead and squeezed off his last round.

The Colt jumped in his hand, spitting a line of orange fire, and a scream erupted below him even as Fargo belly flopped hard on the slope and bounced and rolled the last thirty yards to the bottom, banging into his share of rocks along the way.

Cut, bruised and sore, badly rattled, Fargo nonetheless pushed to his feet as if by reflex alone and exchanged the Colt's empty wheel for the loaded spare. But no more bullets were required: he had caught the rabbit-faced dry-gulcher low in the guts, a long, agonizing death few men could survive in a big city much less the wilderness.

The Spencer's thin barrel had broken off just ahead of the breech when the man fell directly on it. The piercing screams made Fargo wince as he collected the gun belt with its black-gripped Remington and about a dozen shells in the cartridge loops. The man continued screaming—full-throated and hoarse, then high-pitched and piercing—while Fargo stripped his mount and smacked it on the rump, liberating it to a high probability of joining the wild horses common in these parts.

"Fargo!" the man managed between screams. "For God's sake, man, finish me off!"

Usually Fargo did show mercy and toss a finishing shot into mortally wounded foes. But this situation in the Black Hills was desperate, hanging by less than a thread, and he knew those anguished screams were echoing for miles. With luck, Brennan and his two remaining hyenas were listening—and thinking. And it wouldn't hurt if some hotheaded renegades heard them, too.

"You chose to reap the whirlwind," Fargo replied as he began the climb back up to the saddle. "So *reap* it."

Fargo examined the ugly, puckered flesh where the bullet had punched into Logan's emaciated left thigh.

"There're no blood spurts," he said. "That's good—it missed any major arteries."

A hideous, spine-tickling scream sounded on the far side of the saddle between the two hills to their left, repeating itself in diminishing echoes across the Black Hills.

"Hell, Fargo," Logan said, his face twisted against the

excruciating pain in his leg, "why didn't you finish the sewer rat off?"

"If it bothers a coldhearted bastard like you, imagine how the rest of his gang likes it. Damn it, hold still."

"How does it look?"

"Like a bullet in your leg, that's how. If you were up to full fettle I'd dig out that slug and wash the wound with carbolic. Then I'd cauterize it."

"Go ahead and do it."

Fargo shook his head. "Good chance, in your health, it might kill you. I've been through it, and it's a hell-buster."

"Well, if you don't, won't it putrefy and kill me anyway?"

"I'd give that fifty-fifty odds in your poor health. But I'm going to wash it good and pack the wound with beef tallow to stem the bleeding before I wrap it."

"The son of a bitch *hurts*, Fargo. I'm no frontier stoic like you."

"The pain will let up in a day or so. In the meantime . . ."

Fargo dug in a saddlebag and produced a brown bottle labeled Tott's Cordial.

"Take *one* swallow of this," Fargo said. "You can have another swallow every few hours."

"Patent medicine, huh? What is it?"

"Alcohol and laudanum. It dulls the pain, but you won't be much use while you're taking it—not that you're a helluva lot of use anyhow."

"Serve it on toast. That bullet was meant for you, and it was right on bead. It only wounded me because my leg flew up when I was rocked back over my cantle. Otherwise it would have doused *your* glims."

"I got a spooked rabbit to thank, not you," Fargo shot back. "It ain't like you made a choice to take a bullet for me. Damn you, I said *one* swallow."

Fargo snatched the bottle back. After he treated and bandaged the wound, Logan said: "A fifty-fifty chance, huh? Fargo, you know about this stuff. If that leg does mortify, how quick will I know?"

"You should know in the next day or so. It'll hurt worse and itch like hell."

"How long could I survive then?"

"Unless that leg is amputated, maybe three days. But you'd be sick and in a world of pain. And there ain't a snowball's chance you could survive an amputation. If it mortifies, I'd recommend a quick bullet to the brain."

"No need to sugarcoat it," Logan said bitterly. "Fargo, we *have* to work fast now. I'm not leaving this world behind until I kill Stuart."

"I told you this is a job, not a personal grudge match. This hell thirst of yours to kill your brother—has it got anything to do with all the time you spend watching Fort Pierre?"

"We have to work fast," Logan repeated stubbornly, ignoring Fargo's question.

"Once that medicine I gave you kicks in, you'll be worthless. We're riding back to the French Creek camp for a day so you can recruit your strength."

"Like hell! If that wound infects—"

"It ain't up for a vote," Fargo snapped.

"Oh yeah, I get it. It's time for Skye Fargo to get another ration of that fine-haired cunny."

"Targets of opportunity are always welcome," Fargo conceded.

"Yeah? Well, *you're* the one who pushed the 'relentless predator' line, how we have to stay on them like ugly on a buzzard. Going back to French Creek won't accomplish that."

Fargo's lips firmed. "Don't be so sure of that. I been cogitating on that camp, and there's a stink to it I don't like."

By now the alcohol and laudanum were starting to ferry Logan to a more agreeable place. He managed to sit up, wincing only slightly.

"You mean the women?" he asked.

"Among others. Something else is crossways there besides their stories. C'mon, let's get you horsed and point our bridles south."

The moment Fargo fell silent another hideous, almost inhuman scream rent the peace and quiet of the Black Hills, growing hoarse from repetition. Fargo felt no pity and only hoped others were hearing it, too.

But it was also a grim reminder: make one mistake, in this wild and dangerous place, and that could be Skye Fargo's life ending in slow, agonizing death before he was left for carrion.

13

"Hear that, boys?" Stuart Brennan said. "Read 'em and weep."

Another scream, muted by distance, reached them like a summons to their own graves. Brennan, Jack Stubbs and Waco Clayburn had met in a well-hidden cave just north of Blacktail Gulch—one of three they were using.

"Maybe one of us should go plug him," Waco said uncertainly.

Brennan's hard, flat, gunmetal eyes pierced Waco like a pair of bullets. "Are you volunteering?"

Waco frowned and averted his eyes. "Not me. Fargo might expect that and draw down on whoever comes to shoot Dobber."

"You're wising up, Waco. There's no chivalry in our game, boys. It's a rough, dirty business suited only for men willing to kill their own mothers. In the end it boils down to raw mentality, and I'm smarter than Fargo."

The screams were getting weaker, but the awful, terrifying tone was brutally clear. Jack Stubbs was a hard man, and loyal to his boss, but realizing that was a human being making those sounds took the pith out of his legs and forced him to suddenly support himself on the wall of the cave.

"Boss," he said, "I'd stack your gray matter up against any man's. But Fargo always 'pears to be smart enough to deal us misery."

"I *told* you boys right from the jump that Fargo would work on us relentlessly," Brennan admonished them. "You think I talk just to hear myself speak? First a pack mule, now Dobber. And he broke up the second attack Swift Canoe meant to make on the French Creek camp although those renegade bucks did a good job of bloodletting at Spearfish Creek. Word about that will get out to the newspapers and stir up Indian fever. We need more of that."

"I string along with Jack," Waco spoke up, his sullen eyes showing a hint of rebellion. "Fuckin' with Fargo ain't such a bright idea. I say we just leave all the goods for the red arabs and the three of us split up and get shut of these hills."

Brennan looked disgusted, as if he had stepped in dog shit barefooted.

"Is that the female in you talking, Waco?" he demanded. "You don't cut off your arm at the elbow just to get rid of a hangnail."

"Skye Fargo a hangnail? Is that what killed Dobber—a hangnail? I'd say Fargo is more like a six-inch spike in the liver."

"Boss," Jack threw in, "a fellow can lay a feather on a rock and call it a bed, but *I* ain't sleeping in the son of a bitch. I ride for the brand, and I'm sticking if you are. But Fargo ain't no damn hangnail. I'm thinking we need help."

Brennan gave a curt nod of agreement. Despite employing Stubbs for almost a decade now, he despised him. The hard-knit hill man was deferential to money and power. But he was also a perpetual boaster just bursting at the seams to talk himself up mighty high. A know-it-all and trouble-seeking man by nature, good for Brennan's purposes but definitely no match for Skye Fargo.

Brennan said, "You've placed the ax right on the helve, Jack. And we already *have* help—some of the best killers in the world, for starters."

"The Sioux?"

"None other. We've made two mistakes, easily rectified. First, we haven't directly sicced them on Fargo, and second, we've kept them too drunk to best a man of his caliber."

"Yeah," cut in Waco, "but—"

"Stick your 'buts' in your pocket. I cannot abide a whiner."

"I ain't whining, Mr. Brennan, my hand to God I ain't. But this business with counting on the Sioux to kill Fargo . . . you can use gunpowder in place of salt, too, but salt won't fire a rifle."

"Ah, a rhetorician now, are you? Well, you can use sheep in place of a woman, too, but a sheep won't cook your grits. So what's your point?"

"I had one," Waco muttered, "but it skipped my mind."

"Jesus Christ," Stubbs said. "It had to be Dobber we lost instead of *this* thundering idiot."

"As I was explaining before our resident scholar interrupted me, our mistakes are easily remedied. Swift Canoe wants the strong water—*we* want Fargo and Logan Robinson dead. That's an ideal bargain that only needs to be struck."

"Robinson will drop any day now," Stubbs pointed out. "I can't see him as a threat."

For a moment Brennan's face turned somber, even apprehensive. "I told you, Jack, he's a serious threat until he's dead."

"You seem to know something about him, boss."

"His reputation is all any man needs to know," Brennan replied, resuming his usual brusque manner.

"What about that ideal bargain of yours. Mr. Brennan?" Waco asked. "You mean we stop pouring the liquor until the Sioux kill Fargo?"

"Not quite. We can't cut them off completely or they'll explode and kill us. So we cut their ration back and make it clear they'll be pissing rivers of whiskey after they kill Fargo and bring me his head as proof. We can even claim that Fargo is interfering with the whiskey supply."

Stubbs nodded enthusiastically and even Waco had perked up. But he still looked skeptical.

"All that sounds good," he said, "but them Injins ain't stupid. And there ain't no way a man can predict what they'll do. I get the sweats every time you parley with 'em, Mr. Brennan."

"As do I," Brennan agreed. "I only took this job because of the money. And because I know this Indian burner, boys—it's brewed especially to cloud and confuse their thinking and make them hanker hard for more. They'll snap wise soon, but right now it's new and amazing to them and the liquor is our only yoke on them—and the fact they don't know where we hide the ammunition to keep their new thunder sticks in business."

"Yeah-boy, they want that who-shot-John real bad," Stubbs agreed. "That's using your mentality, all right, boss. Now that Fargo has killed Dobber, you want me and Waco to start patrolling?"

Brennan shook his head. "Despite what happened to Dobber I still prefer fixed ambush points. The Sioux will do our patrolling for us. However, I have a new assignment for you two—one that will very quickly let Fargo know his actions have consequences."

He looked at Waco. "Any problem with the prisoners?"

"Nah. They're too scared for their women to pull any parlor tricks."

Brennan nodded. "Both of you need to remember that I always build safeguards into my plans. Those prisoners are a trump card up our sleeves. I take it you boys haven't forgotten that?"

"No," Stubbs said, "but will their women really do it? You know how the calicos lip salt from Fargo's hand."

"He's a notorious womanizer and I imagine they 'lip' various parts of him. But I have faith that lust will not conquer their matrimonial obligations. But that's why we have safeguards—what we lose in herring we'll gain in hake."

"What's 'hake'?" Waco asked.

"Hake," Brennan replied, "is whatever kills Skye Fargo and Logan Robinson."

A few bonfires were burning brightly, flames reflecting yelloworange off the creek, when Fargo and Logan Brennan returned to the French Creek camp.

Fargo had allowed Logan one more swig of Tott's Cordial, and again he had sneaked in a second swallow before Fargo could stop him. He was both drunk and doped up for most of the ride, and twice Fargo had palmed the butt of his Colt, on the verge of shooting the obnoxious assassin.

By journey's end Logan was at the scrag end of his endurance and Fargo, dog tired himself, sent him across the footbridge to the cabin while Fargo let both horses tank up before leading them across the creek and up the wooded slope.

Fargo stripped the leather from both mounts and put them on long ground tethers. The night air was crisp and the horses' manes and coats sweat-matted. Fargo dried both of them off before he headed around to the front of the cabin.

Dad Bodine sat near the door sewing a pair of red longhandles in the glow of a stubby lantern placed on a stump. His

Kentucky long rifle was propped against the cabin within easy reach.

"Dad, you look like somebody just kicked your dog," Fargo greeted him.

"Hell, I've et my pet dogs in starving times, Skye. No, I'm plagued most to death frettin' over them gals. Son, it's plain as cooties on a clean sheet—they ain't nobody a-comin' to fetch 'em."

"Yeah, that gets my money, too. And I suspect they've known that all along."

"Ahuh, I been wondering on that. Hell, I figgered 'em for liars all along. Whatever they're up to, I just hope they get outta here. But the chances for that don't look good."

"I plan to nose into it right now," Fargo said.

"I been fleeced by some slick grifters in my day," Dad said. "But, Skye? It's mighty queer to say it, I know, but I got this gut hunch them gals ain't grifters—somehow they're even more dangerous than that."

"Women are the salt of the earth," Fargo replied. "That's why they drive men to drink."

"The hell happened to that lunger? He staggered into that cabin lookin' like he's ready for the undertaker's rouge."

"He got shot," Fargo said, leaving it there. "How's things been around here?"

Dad didn't just laugh with contempt—he barked. "We're *all* gonna end up with a bullet in our lights happens we don't dust our hocks priddy damn quick. Word come today that a prospectors' camp nigh to Spearfish Creek was catawampously chawed up. Redskins killed the whole damn boodle of 'em."

That news sobered Fargo. He couldn't be every damn place at once especially now that weariness was starting to take its toll on him. But news of that massacre—or so the inkslingers would call it—would get noised around quickly, just as the Indian Ring intended.

It's root hog or die, Fargo reminded himself. Once the Sioux were pushed past the point of no return, it wouldn't matter if Stuart Brennan and his men were killed. The conflagration of war would engulf the Dakota Territory.

"Nothing like gold," Fargo said, "to tangle men's brains."

Dad spat a streamer of 'baccy juice into the brown grass. "Gold, eh? Why, Jesus hell, Skye! Most of these sourdoughs here has got 'em hog troughs full of gold by now. I keep bangin' my gums at 'em 'bout how the old Sioux peace chiefs is being howled down by the younger warriors, how close we are to the reckoning. They nod at me, but like you say, the gold lust has got ahold of their minds."

"It's not just the prospectors riling the Sioux," Fargo said. "There're white men in these hills stirring up the shit for the war profiteers."

"You struck a lode there. I've seed it more'n once. There's always some son of a bitch lower'n a snake's belly in a wagon rut, spurrin' folks to killing others so he can feather his own nest."

Fargo reached for the latchstring to go inside. "Noticed anything new or different about Adrienne and Ursula?"

"They both got the fidgets bad, and the two has took to fightin' between 'em like cooped-up cats."

Fargo let himself inside. His legs were wet and cold from fording French Creek. But a cheery fire on the kitchen hearth had filled the cabin with welcome warmth and mellow light. Logan was already asleep on his pallet, wheezing like a leaky bellows.

Ursula and Adrienne sat at the table drinking tea, again dressed to the nines and pretty as four aces.

"'Home is the hunter, home from the hills,'" Adrienne greeted him with her fetching, hesitant smile.

Ursula's, however, was intimate and enticing. "I've thought fondly of you and our last visit, Skye. I'm *very* happy you're back safe."

"That's good to know," Fargo said. "But tell me something else: what is it you ladies are holding back from me?"

Their sudden smiles were too bright and too seductive. They *should* have looked puzzled and offended, Fargo told himself, if they were innocent.

"Whatever do you mean?" Adrienne said.

"I don't believe I spoke Chinese, pretty lass."

"We've told you the truth," Ursula insisted. "You spoke with Dan Appling and he verified our story."

"There're problems with that story. But there's another problem:

you are two very lovely and refined ladies. You are stuck smack-dab in the middle of some of the most dangerous acreage in America, land claimed by the Sioux as their homeland. You've even been under Indian attack. But *not once* have I heard you fret that this supposed rescue mission—led by your husbands—hasn't arrived yet."

"Why, that's simply not true," protested Adrienne. "Perhaps we just don't do it when you're around."

"Horse apples," Fargo said. "Any woman stranded as you two are would talk of *nothing* but that rescue party. It would be on her mind constantly because it would be her only chance."

"That's all we do talk about, Skye."

"Hmm," Fargo said, holding Adrienne's gaze until she glanced away.

"Skye," Ursula said, "you're calling us liars? Are we criminals, too?"

"Liars, I'd say distinct probability. Criminals? I'm neither up the well nor down on that one."

"I thought you were a gentleman," Ursula pouted.

"I'm a man, darlin', but not all that gentle. What's your connection to Stuart Brennan?"

Fargo deliberately smacked them with the question out of thin air. Ursula, the better actress of the two, seemed unfazed. Adrienne paled for a moment but nodded in support when Ursula replied: "I've never heard the name in my life. Skye, you're being needlessly suspicious and unfair."

Fargo shook his head in frustration. "Both of you hearken and heed: this whole area is a powder keg right now. I don't believe there's any rescue party, and I can't get you out of here until I finish my job. Adrienne?"

Fargo could see that she was having the hardest time meeting his eyes.

"Yes, Skye?"

"Are you two somehow being forced to stay here by Brennan or anyone else?"

"Don't be such a goose!" Ursula took over. "We—"

"I asked Adrienne, not you."

Adrienne took in a deep breath. "No, Skye, we're not. I can understand your suspicion, but our story is true."

Fargo shrugged and then surrendered with a grin. "I never could get a straight answer from a woman. Actually, the ones who lie are the most fun."

"Is Logan badly injured?" Ursula asked, obviously relieved that Fargo had retreated.

"For the shape he's in, yeah. I'm not sure he'll come sassy again."

"Poor man," Adrienne said.

"I'll play no violins for him," Fargo said. "The man's a murderer many times over and still makes his brag about it. He's even hinted he's going to kill me."

"But the two of you are working together."

"Sure, and that means I'll do what I can for him by the rules of the trail. But I don't trust him."

"He may be repentant in his heart and just won't admit it," Adrienne suggested. "After all, he's dying."

Fargo only half succeeded in staving off a yawn. "Could be, I s'pose," he replied indifferently. "I don't have religion, so repentance is lost on me."

"Don't you at least feel sorry for him?" Ursula pressed. "*Look* at him, Skye."

"I do feel a little sorry for him," Fargo admitted. "The man is wasted down to almost nothing, coughs up blood all day, but he just keeps soldiering on. Excuse me, ladies, but I want to take a squint around outside."

Fargo stepped back out into the high-altitude chill.

"Them cottontails come clean?" Dad Bodine demanded.

"I got nothing but spider leavings, Dad."

"Ahh . . . *this* child ain't never found no sign on the breast of a woman. 'Course, the tit alone is quite a comfort."

"It's a start," Fargo agreed. "Any trouble out there?"

"Ain't noticed nothin'. But if them renegades decide to hit this place when they're sober, we won't know it until the first shots."

"The way you say. So you'd best put that light out, old roadster. You're giving them a free target."

"One more button and I will. My dick keeps flipping outta these damn underdrawers and chafing on my britches."

Fargo snorted. "Yeah, that's no place for a blister."

Fargo moved down to the creek and stood listening for at

least five minutes. The water chuckled ceaselessly and the wind seemed to whisper ominous secrets as it fluttered the leaves that hadn't yet dropped.

Fargo crossed the bridge and moved a little farther out, planning to circle the camp.

He flinched when rifle fire suddenly erupted about fifty yards away.

"Hell's a-poppin'!" Dad Bodine roared out. "Let 'er rip!"

Fargo heard the solid detonation of Dad's long rifle. The rifles firing on the camp—Fargo counted two—were repeaters and sustained a long volley. He had located their position by ear and opened up furiously with his Henry.

But they must have spotted his muzzle flash. Only seconds after he opened fire the attackers shifted their beads toward him, and hot lead came screaming in all around him, rattling the brush. One bullet dislodged a chunk of bark and sent it smacking into his forehead. But Fargo stood his ground and levered and fired, making it hot for them.

The moment he let up he heard the sounds of hasty retreat as more weapons opened up from the camp.

Fargo hurried back toward the bridge.

"It's Dad Bodine!" somebody roared out. "He's been shot up bad!"

14

"Hold your fire!" Fargo shouted. "Fargo coming in across the bridge! The two shooters have dusted!"

A half circle of men, some carrying lanterns, all armed, had gathered at the front of the cabin. Among them Fargo recognized Jim West, Dan Appling and the hotheaded red beard named Clancy.

They all stood back somewhat from the two women, who were huddled close over the supine form of Dad Bodine. Even Logan had been drawn outside by the commotion.

Fargo shouldered his way through and knelt close to his fallen friend. Dad was still barely conscious but past any hope. Three slugs snake-holed his scrawny chest, and blood bubbled in a pink froth on his lips.

"Was it featherheads, Skye?" Jim West asked.

"Not likely at all. The silent sneak ambush ain't their gait. Indian warriors want coup feathers, and that means confronting and defeating your enemy close-up. And they don't send out one or two fighters to go up against a whiteskin camp— they attack in larger numbers like they did last time."

Even as a saddened Fargo watched, Dad's eyes began to rapidly lose their focus as the vitality ebbed with his blood. Only moments later the old trapper's ultimate breath rattled in his throat like pebbles trapped in a sluice. Now the eyes were simply two glazed marbles, wide open but seeing nothing.

Fargo noticed that Adrienne, the sensitive lover of poetry and ideas, seemed to be the one most stricken.

"What we just saw," she said in a soft voice that didn't carry past Fargo, Logan and Ursula, "was holy. We just saw a human soul leave its body. It left the husk that imprisoned it.

And now it can soar unrestrained like an eagle, seeing everything it could not when Dad was bound to the earth."

Fargo looked at Logan and said nothing. Adrienne, either honestly or with great dramatic skill, began to softly cry.

"You don't believe that, do you, Skye?" She choked back a sob. "You don't believe that what you just saw was transcendent, do you?"

"Lady, I got no idea what that word means," Fargo told her, "and I'm not in any mood to learn it. I've been forced to kill too many men, and I can't afford to think into it too deep because I'm going to have to kill more. Now you get hold of yourself."

"What's all that whispering up there?" demanded Clancy's belligerent, bullhorn voice.

Fargo straightened to his full six feet and confronted the man, who seemed on the verge of bringing his Greener up to the level. He was an unstable man, and the shooting excitement had set him off again.

"Ursula," Fargo said, "take Adrienne inside and stay with her. Clancy, you bring that muzzle up one more inch and I'll burn you down."

"Skye," Jim West spoke up, "don't pay Clancy no nevermind. He's got a brick in his hat."

"Drunk or sober, Jim, when a man puts me under the gun I don't ask any questions until after I kill him."

"I'm sick and tired of this shit!" Clancy bellowed, trying to rouse the others to his fever pitch. "Who made Fargo our lord and master? We didn't ask him here, did we? He ain't pulling out no color, so what's he doing here? You was all here when that jasper warned us Fargo's been hired by the big bugs to run us off. The very next day, here comes Fargo stickin' his oar in *our* boat!"

A few men murmured assent. Clancy pointed a thick index finger at Dad's corpse. "Some of you others seen it just like I done: right after the shootin' Fargo crosses the bridge into camp. Where was he?"

"There were at least two shooters," Jim West reminded him.

"All right, then. Where's the lunger?"

Ursula, listening from the doorway, spoke up. "He was asleep in the cabin."

"Like hob!" Clancy snarled. "You boys seen and heard it— Fargo and them women talking real low right when Dad bucked out. He was telling them what to say!"

Some of the men were considering all this and regarding Fargo with a stony silence. Fargo glanced at Logan and the consumptive nodded the all ready.

Under territorial law Clancy was not just accusing Fargo and Logan of murder—he was clearly on the verge of inciting others to a vigilante execution of them. For this reason Fargo had every right to a call-down, but the situation here was too precarious. Killing a prospector on the heels of Dad's murder would only strengthen the perception that Fargo was on a mission to drive these men out.

If Clancy pushed things too far and Fargo had to kill him, he wanted to make it clear to the rest of these men that his hand was forced.

"Red Beard," Fargo said in an even voice, "if you're accusing me of murder, spell that charge out plain in front of witnesses and then prove it."

Fargo's dangerous tone set Clancy back on his heels.

"I ain't making that an accusation," he replied. "Not yet. Will you let me sniff your rifle?"

"*I'll* let you sniff my asshole," Logan cut in. "And then I'll spray your brains all over that cabin."

"Pretty smart, ain't you, lunger?" Clancy shot back.

"No. It just seems that way to stupid men like you."

"Butt out," Fargo snapped at him. He looked at Clancy again.

"I don't give up my weapons, but I just fired my Henry at the attackers, so you don't need to sniff it."

Clancy glanced around at the men as if he had just proved what the moon was made of.

"I own a Henry, too," spoke up a prospector at the fringe of the flickering light. "And I recognized at least one shootin' at *us*."

"That's right," Fargo said, "because one of those yellow dogs had a Henry. The other sounded like a Spencer."

"Does them use different cartridges?" Clancy demanded.

"Very different," Fargo affirmed.

"All right, then! We'll haul Dad's body down to the saloon

tent and dig them bullets out. If they ain't from a Henry, Fargo's in the clear."

Funny, Fargo thought. According to his friend Jim West, Dan Appling was the leader of the prospectors. But he was holding back with the others, letting Eric the Red here play the big Indian.

"I'm in the clear now," Fargo said. "And what if it *is* a bullet from a Henry? I've seen at least two in this camp, and right now the Sioux are being supplied with Henrys and Spencers."

"If it ain't from a Henry," Clancy persisted stubbornly, "you got nothing—"

"Clancy, hush down!" Jim West snapped. "Fargo's got nothing to prove. He's no damn murderer and I'll vouch for that."

"No, go ahead and carve those bullets out," Fargo said. "I'm curious to see what old Clancy has plans to do if those slugs *did* come from a Henry."

"I'll do what needs to be done," Clancy boasted.

"Knock yourself out—it's your funeral," Fargo assured him right back.

Dad's body was placed on a board and four men hauled him off. Fargo and Logan trailed the others toward the saloon tent. Logan noticeably favored his left leg. Most of the Tott's Cordial had worn off and he was clearly in pain.

"We'd better kill Clancy," Logan muttered. "These prospectors are on the feather edge of turning their guns on us, and that loudmouth is the one egging them on."

"Bad idea," Fargo differed. "He deserves it, all right, but we'll kill only if our hand is forced. We kill him and the rest will turn us into sieves unless we slaughter the whole pack."

"We can do that," Logan boasted. "If we each drop six of them fast enough—"

"Only if we're forced to it," Fargo repeated. "I know killing is like taking a woman for you, but we were hired to lock horns with your brother, not slaughter prospectors. Hell, you can't blame them for being suspicious."

"Yeah? Well pin *this* to your hat: if you're squeamish that's your problem. I'm the Missouri Mad Dog and *I'm* the one who decides who I'm going to kill and when."

Fargo wasn't interested right then in a pissing contest. Something else was troubling him. Moments ago Dan Appling had summarily appointed himself as Dad Bodine's replacement to guard the women and he had stayed behind at the cabin.

"Do you find it a mite too coincidental," he asked Logan, "that earlier today I killed one of your brother's dirt workers, and now Dad Bodine is cut down—almost like it was immediate retaliation?"

"Now that you mention it, yeah, I do think it's a queer deal. If not, why'd they select that old man—a longtime friend of yours?"

"Somehow," Fargo speculated, "your brother seems to know what's going on at this camp. While you were sleeping I mentioned his name to the women. And I'm convinced Adrienne recognized the name."

"If that's true," Logan said, "then that whole song and dance about Appling rescuing them is sheep dip."

"Yeah. And it likely means Appling is on your brother's payroll."

"You think the women are, too?"

"That's a poser," Fargo admitted.

"Well, we've got a more immediate problem," Logan pointed out. "What happens if those slugs in the old rooster *were* fired from a Henry?"

"Then it's up to Red Beard and the hotheads who side with him. Like I said, if we're forced to it we'll kill as many as we have to."

"That's more like it," Logan approved. "But what about that loner Cheyenne who jumped you in your bedroll? You say Indians don't favor the hidden ambush, but you called him a . . . what, a cantankerous warrior?"

"A *contrary* warrior if that's what he is."

"If he's 'contrary' wouldn't that mean he breaks the rules?"

"Maybe," Fargo conceded, "but there were two shooters. Still, I wonder what the hell that buck's up to."

By the time the two men reached the tent, Jim West, his face grim at the distasteful task, was already at work using a case knife to dig the bullets out. A former gunsmith known as Bearcat Jones stood beside him waiting.

"Slide around behind me," Fargo muttered to Logan, "and be ready to put your back to mine. If this deal goes south on us, we want two directions covered when we throw down."

West pried the first slug out, wiped it off on Dad's shirt, and handed it to Jones.

"Never mind the expert opinion," Fargo told the assembled men. He pulled a taper-cased brass cartridge from his possibles bag. "This is the round fired by a Henry: four hundred eighty grains of powder and the bullet is the exact diameter and length of the one in Bearcat's hand. I can see it from here—that slug was likely fired from a Henry."

"'At's right," Bearcat confirmed. "It definitely ain't no Spencer round."

Bearcat's words seemed to hang in the air like a guilty verdict.

"Well, boys, if that don't cap the climax!" Clancy burst out. "I say we—"

"Shut your cake-hole," Logan cut him off. "Fargo isn't a murderer because he's got 'scruples.' I've got none and cold-blooded killing rolls right off my back. Right now your tongue is a shovel, and you're about to dig your own grave with it if you don't sing soft."

Physically, Logan was a pathetic, weak sight. His clothing sagged from his emaciated body, and it seemed to require all of his strength just to keep his balance. But his skullish face—almost a literal death's head—and disease-ravaged, sheening eyes were unnerving. And most of the men assembled here knew his reputation.

Clancy's fingers worked nervously on the stock and twin barrels of his scattergun. Building up his guts to use it, Fargo realized, and most likely he would. Fargo knew what was coming and stayed out of it.

"You disgusting little freak," Clancy growled. "Playin' cock o' the walk while the Reaper is pulling you under. That bitch lied at the cabin—you was *with* Fargo when you two killed Dad Bodine. You're a low-down, shit-eating, murdering coward, and I'm telling you that to your ugly pan."

"Compliment received, noted and accepted," Logan said. "But I told you to pipe down."

Clancy, a foolish man whose mouth outran his brain,

started to raise his Greener. Fargo barely saw the draw when Logan cleared leather. The Navy barked once and a rope of blood spurted from Clancy's left eye. Logan's second shot punctured the right eye, putting two bullets in Clancy's brain in less than a second. He belly flopped to the packed-dirt floor, already dead before he landed.

"Sainted backsides!" one of the startled men exclaimed.

"What do you expect for two bits?" Logan inquired of the assembly as he leathered his shooter.

"Hold your powder, boys!" Jim West shouted. "This jasper may be a notorious murderer, but *this* ain't murder. I saw them barrels coming up and the kill light in Clancy's eyes."

"Me, too," Bearcat put in. "It was self-defense."

"Lissenup, boys," West added. "Dad Bodine always bragged about his friendship with Fargo. He was proud as a game rooster 'bout it. And Fargo told me once that Dad was one of the old trappers who taught him how to survive on the frontier. *Why* would Fargo kill an old man who ain't even a prospector instead of, say, Clancy, who's been hot-jawin' Fargo and making trouble? It don't make sense nohow."

"Admit it, boys," Logan said, fingers trembling as he thumbed in two reloads. "You're *glad* he's gone to glory. Now you can all go shares on the stupid galoot's gold."

"Bottle it," Fargo told him although it was the truth. He addressed the others.

"Gents, think about it before more men die. If me and Robinson were being paid to drive you out, why would we need to show ourselves to you? We're both crack shots. We could stay in hiding and kill a dozen of you before you could even get out of the creek. Why in hell would we face your wrath like this if we don't have to?"

"I believe you, Mr. Fargo," Bearcat said. "I have since you first rode in here. But it don't help none that you won't tell us why you *are* here."

"Yeah, and showing up with him," one of the men tossed in, nodding toward Logan. "Since when does the Trailsman ride with murderers?"

"I'm here on your behalf, boys, and that's straight arrow. I didn't pick Robinson—my employer did. And I'll tell you this much: we've been sent to stop an Indian war before they lift every paleface scalp in this region. That war is only a fox step away."

"Clancy was always spoiling for trouble," said one of the prospectors. "And he was always going off half-cocked. Fargo's right: the Trailsman is too damn smart to create trouble he could easy avoid."

The tension soon broke. It was late and these hardworking men were tired. They began to file out.

"Hey, you pikers!" West called out. "We got two bodies to bury."

"I'll take care of Dad right now," Fargo said. "Me and him go back a ways."

"And I'll pray over the grave," West volunteered. "I know that ain't in your line, Skye."

Fargo looked at Logan. "From the look of you, maybe I should dig two graves. Get some shut-eye."

"I can't sleep—this damn leg is giving me jip."

"I'll give you another slug of the laudanum before I bury Dad. But I'm holding a gun to your head, and if you guzzle it this time you'll never finish the second swallow."

"You think these prospectors still mean to kill us?" Logan asked.

"At the moment, no. But they're spooked and we'll need to watch our ampersands. Anyhow, we'll be out of here at first light. You made the right call with Clancy—and popping his eyeballs out like you did shocked the fight out of the others. But we're on thin ice everywhere, Mad Dog, and it's going to get thinner."

15

Fargo dug Dad Bodine's grave on a grassy bench beside the creek, where unobstructed moonlight cast just enough illumination for him to see what he was doing.

The prospectors who helped carry Dad's body waited respectfully until he was in the earth and West had finished the Lord's Prayer.

"Jim," Fargo said when the others had drifted back to their bedrolls, "how well do you know Dan Appling?"

"Well, he got here in the spring and that's the first time I met him. Why?"

"Just curious. I know that you prospectors try to stay in groups when you leave camp. Does Appling ride out much by himself?"

"Why . . . I don't think so," West replied. "'Cept he does ride out hunting for fresh meat regular-like."

"You've been a prospector for years. How many sourdoughs have you known who regularly take time off from their claims to hunt?"

West was silent for at least ten seconds while the creek murmured nearby. Somewhere in the folds of forested mountains a puma screamed, and when the wind blew, cold knifed into both men.

"Yeah, I catch your drift, Skye. Most men will eat dirt pies before they'll take time off from panning to hunt. And, you know, when I recollect back on it—sometimes he's gone for hours, but he never comes back with more'n a few quail or a couple rabbits. And, hell, there's a fat deer behind every tree in the Black Hills. I've shot a few without even leaving the creek. You know what game is like in these mountains."

West looked at Dad's unmarked grave, which the two men had covered with rocks to keep predators off.

"All right, Skye," he said, "what do you know?"

"Keep this dark from the others," Fargo replied, "because I got no solid proof. But I got a strong hunch that Appling *might* be in cahoots with the graveyard rats who are stirring the Sioux up for war."

"Jesus!"

"Even worse, I think Adrienne and Ursula are in it with him."

It took West several seconds to recover from a stunned silence. "Those two beautiful ladies—*criminals*?"

"I don't go that far, not yet. But you'd be wise to keep an eye on them *and* Appling."

By the time Fargo returned to the cabin atop the rise he was dog tired.

"Who goes there?" challenged a voice in the darkness.

"It's Fargo."

"Howdy, Mr. Fargo," Appling's disembodied voice greeted him.

Fargo could just make out his shadowy form in Dad's old spot—a three-legged stool beside the door. He was wrapped in a blanket, and Fargo felt a cold lick along his spine when he realized Appling's rifle seemed to be pointed at him.

"I'd 'preciate it all to hell and back," Fargo told him, "if you wouldn't point that smoke wagon at me."

"Sorry. It wasn't deliberate."

"No need to freeze your ass off out here," Fargo told him. "I'll be sleeping in the cabin."

"I don't mind guard duty. I sleep real good sittin' up."

Fargo always favored the element of slap-in-the-face surprise, and he employed it now after moving his right palm to the butt of his Colt.

"Tell me, Dan: how do you like working for Stuart Brennan?"

The wind gusted, stirring the remaining leaves. Finally:

"You lost me there, Mr. Fargo. I don't know anybody named Stuart Brennan."

The damn liar took too long to answer, Fargo thought, and his voice is too tight.

"Could be I was misinformed," Fargo said sarcastically.

"Obviously you're a scrubbed angel. Now go on back to your she-bang."

"I don't mind sitting—"

"I *do* mind," Fargo cut him off, his voice hardening. He thumb-cocked his revolver as he shucked it out. "And in the morning I recommend you gather up your nuggets and put the Black Hills way behind you."

"Fargo, who in Sam Hill do you think you are to run me off? Whatever you're accusing me of, what's your proof for it?"

"Now, see, that's where you're a damn lucky man. By sending you packing I'm giving you a chance to live. Because I'm soon going to *get* that proof, and the moment I do you're gonna be picking lead out of your liver. Savvy that?"

Fargo had not taken his eyes off that rifle. He detected a wavering movement of the barrel.

"If that weapon moves one more inch toward me," Fargo promised in a low, flat voice, "it's a long, cold rest for you. Now hand it to me stock first."

Appling surrendered the rifle, a six-shot revolving-cylinder Colt, and Fargo emptied the wheel, tossing the cartridges off into the trees.

"Dust," Fargo ordered, handing the weapon back. "I didn't like you the first second I laid eyes on you. You're one of these conniving bastards who shows too many teeth when he smiles. I think you'd kill a man for his boots."

"Fargo, *I'm* the big he-bear around here. The men are going to hear about this, and you're the one who—*unh!*"

Fargo backhanded the man so hard that he knocked him off the stool.

"Threaten me one more time, curly wolf—just *one* more time—and you'll be shoveling coal in hell. I guarandamntee it. Jim West is the big he-bear now, and I just took him to school about you. Those 'hunting trips' of yours were meetings with Brennan or his men. I'm giving you this one chance to find a healthier climate. And unless you're stupider than God made you, you'll find it quick."

Appling struggled to his feet and headed down the slope without another word. Fargo kept him under the gun until the shadowy form was absorbed by the night.

Fargo let himself into the welcome warmth of the cabin and pulled the latchstring in behind him.

Logan, his breathing shallow and rapid, was in deep, drug-induced sleep on his pallet beside the door. Fargo could faintly hear the bubbling mucus and sputum that was rapidly building up in his lungs and would eventually suffocate him—assuming that leg wasn't already mortifying and ended up killing him first.

"*There* you are," Ursula greeted him. "Logan told us what happened at the saloon tent. I made you something to help you sleep."

"I don't think I'll need much help, cupcake."

Fargo, limbs heavy with weariness, propped his Henry against a side wall after making sure the chamber was clear. He stopped in his tracks, transfixed by Ursula's big, honey-colored eyes and the burnished-gold penumbra where the flattering firelight backlit her hair. She was dressed for bed in a thin linen wrapper.

"Well, now," he greeted her, "if *you* aren't a tonic for tired eyes."

"Oh, pouf! I might value that compliment," she teased him, "if I didn't know you were a notorious womanizer."

"A busy bee samples many flowers," he replied in a guilty-as-charged voice.

"Well, I for one am grateful you are so experienced. Practice makes perfect, and Skye Fargo, you were perfect the other night. It takes my breath away just recalling it."

"Yeah, well you're no slouch, either. I take it Adrienne has turned in?"

"Not exactly—I mean I doubt if she's asleep. She's been in her bed sobbing off and on since poor Dad Bodine was killed. Here, try this."

She took a small pan off the hearth and poured a gleaming amber concoction into a pottery mug. "It's a toddy," she explained. "Brandy mixed with hot water and sugar. Logan loved it."

"A toddy? Sounds a mite old-maidish," Fargo said in a dubious tone as he sat at the table. He took a tentative sip. "Say"—he approved—"I must be an old maid—tastes delicious."

"I heard you outside talking to Dan Appling," she remarked a bit too casually. "Did I hear you two arguing?"

Fargo narrowed his eyes shrewdly over the rim of his cup. "That bothers you, does it?"

"Yes!" she replied with surprising force. "I wish you had killed him."

"Why?"

"I . . . Oh, I don't like him, that's all."

"Kinda surprises me," Fargo said, still watching her closely. "I mean, what with him saving you two gals when your coach smashed up, right?"

"Yes, of course."

"Well, your husbands should be here any day to rescue you. I'm sure you're looking forward to that?"

She only nodded to this. "Skye?"

"Hmm?"

Ursula glanced over his shoulder at the blankets dividing the single room. "I'm sure poor Adrienne could use some . . . comforting. She's quite sensitive, you know—quite *passionate*? Dad Bodine's death has greatly upset her."

"Comforting?" Fargo drained the cup and set it down, recognizing an interesting turn in the trail.

"You know what I mean. We're both very attracted to you. And sometimes, when a woman is under terrible duress, she needs to stop thinking—needs to be physically diverted from emotional turmoil."

Fargo said nothing to this string of thirty-five-cent words, just watching her. Ursula decided to be more direct.

"Skye, she asked me to send you into her. Adrienne wants to go the limit with you. Don't worry about me—I'll remain out here."

"She asked?" he clarified.

"Quite clearly."

"And Adrienne the poet used those words: 'go the limit'?"

"Well, no, I used those words. It's just a manner of speaking."

"A manner of speaking," Fargo inquired, "bound to get a man instantly excited—which it did, by the way."

"My goodness, are you a lawyer parsing words now? However she said it, certainly you would enjoy it?"

"I always do," he assured her. "But I'm a mite surprised to find out she has such a pretty pimp."

She flushed and her lips tightened with indignation. "That's cruel, Skye."

"Yeah, it was," Fargo conceded. "Mainly I wanted to see your reaction, not offend you."

Both of these women were top-shelf beauties. And certainly other married women had given him the come-hither. But even Fargo's perennial lust didn't blind him to the fact that something was way off-kilter here—until the sudden stirring of his manhood began to rob his brain of blood and he no longer cared.

"With me it's always the woman's choice," he said, unfolding to his feet.

Ursula couldn't miss the tent in his trousers. "I see you're amenable. Just go on back there—I'm sure she's awake and expecting you."

Fargo stopped in the narrow opening near the back wall. Several candles burned in a pewter holder, and his first glimpse of Adrienne made him forget his next breath.

She lay atop the bedcover, a stricken look on her pretty face. She wore only a chemise of thin muslin—so thin he could trace the dark, swollen protuberances of her nipples. The chemise had ridden high up on her legs, so scandalously high that Fargo glimpsed a raven-black triangle of silky hair before she tugged the chemise lower and sat up.

"Oh! Skye, I don't mean to appear so wanton."

Fargo had been momentarily bolted in place by the erotic vignette before him.

"Funny, I don't feel offended," he assured her, stepping closer to the bed of leather webbing. "But I can't guarantee you're safe from my 'unbridled lust.'"

Fargo got that choice phrase from *Skye Fargo, Frontier Slayer*, the popular chronicle that told the "true story" of the Trailsman and put him on a white stallion named Comet.

"I don't *want* to be safe from it," she told him in a breathy voice.

Boldly, she pulled the chemise up to her navel and spread her shapely, ivory-smooth thighs wider apart. The soft folds and petals of her most intimate place glistened like a coral grotto in the candlelight. With two fingers she tugged back on the chamois-soft hood, bringing her pearl nubbin into view.

"Damn," Fargo said. "Now, this is something like it."

"Will you help me stop worrying for a bit, Skye?" she pleaded. "I know I'm shameless, but tonight I want it so much."

Fargo swallowed audibly as he unbuckled his gun belt and dropped it near the bed. "Any favor for a lady. Let's get thrashing."

He dropped his buckskin trousers to his knees and Adrienne's forget-me-not blue eyes widened at the hefty sight. His staff seemed to possess a life of its own as it leaped ravenously with every beat of his heart. This exciting sight of raw, lustful masculinity mesmerized her like a bird tranced by a snake.

"Oh, my stars," she said in an urgent whisper. "Ursula told me, but I thought she was exaggerating."

Fargo started to lower himself into his favorite saddle, but Adrienne wrapped a hand tightly around his gland and said, "Wait, Skye . . . the first one is always too fast. Let me relieve the pressure and then we can have a long one. Roll onto your side."

Fargo so loved it when women ordered him around in bed. He obliged her and she slid down, bending his staff just right. Fargo released an approving moan when wet, tight heat flowed over his arousal as she took him into her mouth.

She began by swirling her tongue around the sensitive dome, flicking rapidly and sending a delicious current of hot and tickling pleasure all the way down to his groin. His reaction triggered hers, and soon her head was plunging back and forth like a steam piston in feverish abandon as she took as much of him as she could into the moist snugness of her mouth.

Fargo held off as long as his will allowed him, but his resistance crumbled when she began to rake her teeth along the underside. An overwhelming surge of pleasure blacked out his mind and swelled him to an iron hardness. Fargo's entire body twitched out of control before he exploded over and over, spending himself and gasping for air.

He was still adrift in that dazed weakness that always followed intense release when Adrienne's sudden outcry jolted him awake.

"No, Ursula, *no*, we can't do it!"

Fargo pushed up on one elbow and glanced toward the opening in the wall of blankets.

He felt ice water replace his blood when Ursula drew back the hammer of a Colt Pocket Model. Her pretty face was a mask of grim determination.

"We *have* to, Adrienne," she replied, curling her finger around the trigger. "We just *have* to!"

16

Fargo's mind was a confused riot of thoughts as he stared at the unblinking eye of the gun. Here was the Damned Thing at last, the buck-out, the end of his trail. His very first reaction was irritation that he hadn't got a longer crack at this hot little lynx beside him.

But his mind turned serious in a heartbeat. His own Colt was within awkward reach, and the Arkansas toothpick was obstructed by the trousers now bunched around his ankles like banana peels.

But her gun was on him, a finger on the trigger, and nothing was faster than a bullet. His survival instincts calculated without thought and told him that any defensive reaction would be futile and would surely provoke Ursula to shoot even sooner.

Whistling past the graveyard, Fargo teased, "Well, a second ago I was coming and now I'm going."

His poor joke was wasted on Ursula, who didn't seem to have heard him. Her hand was trembling as she screwed up her courage to kill.

Jesus, Fargo fretted. A shaker . . . the most dangerous kind when there was no more trigger slack.

"We must do it, Adrienne," she told her friend. "You know that killing him is our only hope—our only choice."

To Fargo it sounded more like she was trying to convince herself. He spoke up quickly.

"You got that bass-ackwards, lady," he assured her. "I'm your only hope, not Stuart Brennan's 'word of honor.' That low-down son of a bitch would toss a drowning man both ends of the rope. He's holding your husbands prisoner, isn't he?"

"Never mind!" Ursula snapped, her face a study in abject

misery. "I'm going to shoot him now, Adrienne, before my courage fails."

"No! Skye is right. . . . We can't trust Brennan and you know it. After we kill Skye, Brennan and his criminal pigs will rape and then kill us. They may already have killed Larry and Arthur."

Ursula's hand trembled even harder and Fargo's back broke out in clammy sweat. The way she was shaking, that damn gun was about to go off whether she intended it or not. One thing Fargo never cared to be was a "death by misadventure," the term used to dismiss any woman who killed a man in the West.

"Ursula," he bluffed, "either pull that damn trigger or lower that weapon. Or do you plan to let the suspense kill me?"

Her finger moved almost imperceptibly as it took up a little more trigger slack. Fargo felt some of his masculine equipment roll under the porch.

"Then again," Fargo amended when she called his bluff, "don't let me rush you."

"Ursula, don't do it!" Adrienne commanded.

"Ursula," he said, desperate to reach her, "you're about to shoot a hole in your own canoe. Logan and me were sent here to kill Brennan, and earlier today I killed one of his men—just for starters. Adrienne's right, there's a good chance your husbands are already dead. But maybe not, and anyway, why should you die, too?"

Another long, agonizing ten seconds or so passed like an eternity, Fargo's fate literally in the hands of a beautiful, scared, confused woman. Then Ursula suddenly burst into tears and lowered the weapon. Fargo sneaked his trousers up.

"Skye, how did you know?" Adrienne asked.

"I didn't know for sure, but I've seen it before and you two fit the pattern. What happened?"

"Part of our lie is true. Butterfield sometimes books up to four passengers on its mail coaches. The four of us boarded in Saint Louis. Somewhere east of here we were attacked by four men, one of them Dan Appling."

"And they killed the driver and shotgun?"

She nodded. "First they shot them with guns and then they shot arrows into them."

"Yeah, that's common out here. Putting it on the renegades makes for a perfect crime, especially since the featherheads got nothing against killing palefaces and do it all the time."

"And, Skye? Afterward they . . . they—"

"Scalped them," Fargo finished for her.

"Oh, Skye!" Ursula spoke up, coming in and sitting on the other bed. "It was just awful! I have nightmares about it. Appling made all four of us watch while they did it. When they ripped the scalps off, they made this horrid sound like hundreds of bubbles popping."

Fargo glanced at her and answered with mild irony. "Yeah, well, I see you haven't buried the memory yet."

He looked at Adrienne again. "Did Brennan actually speak to you two?"

"We've never seen him and didn't know his name until you spoke it, surprising us with it. We knew there was a 'boss' because we overheard the men."

"Any idea where they took your husbands?"

Adrienne shook her head. "Our orders were to seduce you, one of us killing you while the other . . . pleasured you. Oh, Skye, *might* our husbands still be alive?"

"Why not? No way, though, Brennan will set the four of you free—you're all witnesses against him, and his kind doesn't leave witnesses. But taking hostages on the frontier has distinct advantages to sage rats, and you two are smart enough to take my drift."

"We expected to be ravaged, of course," Adrienne said. "These men aren't even distant cousins of the human race."

"There's a chance they've kept your husbands alive," Fargo suggested, "to make you two more cooperative when they rape you. And this whole rescue plan story: pure bunkum, right?"

Adrienne nodded. "That was another reason why they needed Appling. He had to be in charge of the rescue lie so you wouldn't be so suspicious about our being here."

"Do you think Appling's part of the gang?"

"It doesn't appear so," Ursula replied. "The other three treated him as a hired outsider, a menial. It was his job to get us into camp with that phony version of the stagecoach incident. And to keep reminding us our husbands' lives were on the line."

"And keep an eye on you and Logan," Adrienne added. "Somehow they knew you were coming."

"Yeah. From what I hear of him, this Stuart Brennan spreads his money around like manure and has a lot of informers."

"Where are you going?" Ursula said when Fargo buckled on his gun belt and clapped his hat on.

"It was only strong suspicion before," Fargo replied. "Now I know all about Dan Appling. I warned him to pull up stakes real soon, but now I know he's too dangerous to leave alive."

"You mean you're going to *kill* him?" Adrienne exclaimed.

"You want me to powder his butt and tuck him in? He's a murderer and a kidnapper, a real threat to us, and in case you ladies haven't noticed, there's no court and jails anywhere near us."

"Remember, Adrienne," Ursula put in, "the man *does* work for Brennan, after all. Skye's right: there's no telling how he could still hurt us."

"I understand, but what if Brennan retaliates by killing Larry and Arthur—I mean, if they're still alive?"

Fargo mulled that. He recalled his suspicion that Dad Bodine was murdered in retaliation for Brennan's gunny Fargo killed earlier that day.

"Good point. I wouldn't say it's likely, but I can't rule it out, either. And maybe it's smarter not to tip Brennan off. I'll hold off and hope Appling is as scared as he looked outside. If so, he'll make tracks out of the Black Hills in the morning."

"Skye," Ursula said, "it's the Sioux you're worried about too, isn't it?"

"Only a fool wouldn't be. It's not just a matter of killing Brennan and his filthy hyenas. The real challenge is killing them before the entire Sioux Nation explodes."

Two hours after sunup Fargo and Logan cleared the tree cover of a peak in the northeastern quadrant of the Black Hills.

The air here was chilly and bracing, the view of granite spires, splashing creeks and multicolored forests impressive. Fargo watched a peregrine falcon soar high on a wind current. The peace and beauty was an odd match to the violence of these mountains.

Fargo had checked Logan's leg before the men rode out,

and he'd found no signs yet of infection. The pain, too, was dulling, but Logan was in a sullen mood because Fargo had denied him any more Tott's Cordial.

"Do I get to know your secret plans, general?" he spoke up after a long silence. "Or am I too close to the grave to count?"

Fargo found it hard to believe that Logan was still able to slog on in his weak condition. Fargo himself, despite a hot meal and a few hours' sleep last night, was rapidly flagging after too many hard days and too little sleep. This deal was dragging on too damn long, and Fargo knew time favored Stuart Brennan's war-making machine.

"Why bother telling you?" Fargo replied. "You'll likely ignore it. You've got your own plan and you've had it since we rode out from Fort Pierre. Your plan is to be the one to kill your brother, and that's all."

"True, but perhaps I can fit that into your planning if you tell me what it is."

"There're only a few things I can think of to do," Fargo replied. "We can catch them again on the supply trail, which I figure they keep shifting. We can find where Brennan and his men hole up. But seeing's how they keep moving around, that's a tall order when time is pressing. Moving back and forth in this terrain ain't exactly like rolling off a log especially when you're searching it."

"No, but if that savage was telling the truth, you don't have to search much for those caves. I like the idea of going at the caves. Close-quarter killing is my favorite."

"It's not up for a vote," Fargo reminded him, "but we just might do that. We could also stake out this corner of the Black Hills where they give way to the plains. That's the likely spot where they break out of the hills to parley with the Sioux. But that's the problem—the Sioux. Too many too close. Whatever we do, we can't let up on your brother."

Logan said, "Why don't they all just parley in the hills where they're safer and nobody can see them?"

"Even very few of the renegades would work deals with white men in their *Paha Sapa*. That would jinx them and the place."

Logan coughed for about ten seconds, his ashen face shading toward purple for a few moments.

"Over in London and Paris," he said weakly, "they call American Indians noble savages. All these sacred places and customs, all this smearing themselves with blood and paint, yet I guess they're too damn 'noble' to harness the wheel or write their languages down."

"Tell you what," Fargo said, "you can ask this one all about it to his face. But *don't* jerk steel. He's not attacking—yet."

"Who in the hell are you—?"

Logan's jaw slacked open when he spotted the warrior who had just emerged from the trees onto the narrow trace about fifteen feet ahead.

Fargo made the "cut-arm" sign by drawing his hand across his arm like a knife. He was telling the brave he recognized him as a Cheyenne.

"Speak paleface?" Fargo called to him.

"Paleface maybe so."

"I know you," Fargo said, finally getting a good look at the brave who had spied on and attacked him.

His face was shrewdly handsome with the high, finely sculpted cheekbones and even, pleasing features that had earned the Cheyenne tribe the name "the Beautiful People" from neighboring tribes. But this one's features were severely marred by a deep, livid scar—made, Fargo had heard, by a Pawnee war ax—that ran from just below his left ear to the right point of his jaw.

"Maybe so know you," the brave replied. "Far-go."

The Cheyenne's name was Wolf Who Hunts Grinning, and he was indeed an infamous contrary warrior Fargo had heard of for some time. But the Trailsman avoided saying the name— many tribes believed their names lost their power when spoken in front of white men.

"So this is an untutored bachelor of the forest close-up," Logan remarked. "I have to admit he's fierce, but he needs to work on that haircut."

"He's a contrary warrior," Fargo said. "A loner. He cuts his hair short that way to defy the tribe. Fights by his own rules and follows no chiefs. Being a loner is nothing to a one-man outfit like you or me. But it's mighty rare to find a Cheyenne who's left his tribe to live alone."

The warrior looked at Logan, keeping his face blank as a

granite slab. Only women and white men were weak enough to reveal feelings in their faces.

"Maybe so squaw fight better," he said, unable to keep the contempt from his voice as he looked at the weak, dying man.

Fargo pointed at the brave, then himself. "Why attack Fargo?"

The Cheyenne pointed at Fargo's boot. "Knife. Only want parley."

"I guess he's saying he had to jump me once I pulled my knife," Fargo told Logan. "And he's right. Says he only wanted to talk with me."

He nodded at the brave. "Why parley Fargo?"

Wolf Who Hunts Grinning drew a hand across his forehead—it symbolized the tan lines made by white men's hats.

"Paleface dogs! Maybe so make war. Lakota, yellow eyes, all war!"

"He's figured out," Fargo translated for Logan, "that some white men are trying to start a war between the Sioux and the prospectors."

"Who are the yellow eyes?"

"He calls the prospectors that because so many have jaundice."

The brave seemed impatient that they were talking when he had important things to say. "Maybe so make bad medicine Wakan Tanka."

"That's the Cheyenne name for these hills," Fargo told Logan. "Means Great Mystery. It ain't just the Sioux who value this place. See how all the arrows in his parfleche are painted blue? That stands for the Cheyennes' secret, sacred lake somewhere around here. He fears Brennan's bunch has brought bad medicine to the place."

"Swift Canoe," the contrary warrior said, meaning the Hunkpapa leader of the Sioux renegades currently in the area. "No firewater, maybe so brave warrior. Drink strong water, mean dog. War come soon. White dogs, Swift Canoe, yellow eyes. War soon."

The brave pretended to drink. "Strong water, war come. Maybe so one sleep, two sleep."

Fargo nodded agreement. "You fight white dogs?"

Wolf Who Hunts Grinning solemnly shook his head.

"Fight better not maybe. Five sleeps, see sun-moon. Bad medicine. Die water."

"The hell's that gibberish all about?" Logan asked.

"Five days ago," Fargo said, "he saw a dreaded omen: the moon was still visible in the sky when the sun rose. Because he saw it here in the Black Hills, he takes it personally. He believes that omen means an unclean death by drowning if he fights your brother."

"Sounds to me like he's just scared and making an excuse."

Fargo shook his head. "Look at his coup feathers and battle scars. I've heard of him, and once I saw him in action against the Crow tribe. He's a top-notch fighter. He picks his own battles, and he fights to win. But no warrior bucks an omen seen in the Black Hills."

"Fargo kill dogs," the Cheyenne ordered. "Soon maybe so better. Soon war."

Fargo nodded. "Maybe so Fargo kill white dogs."

Again the Cheyenne made the symbol for white men before holding up two fingers. Then he made the dipping-finger sign.

"Brennan has two prisoners," Fargo interpreted from a string of hand signals. "Brennan's bunch uses three . . . Three what? Three caves."

The warrior pointed toward a cataract foaming on a distant slope. Fargo recognized the massacre site called Chinaman's Chance.

"Cave water," the brave said. He turned to the south and pointed at Blacktail Gulch, visible from here. "Cave."

Now he pointed due east toward towering Bear Butte out on the surrounding plains.

"One cave, priss-nur," the Cheyenne said.

He made a wavy motion and then a straight slash. When Fargo nodded his understanding, the brave spread his arms wide like a bird and then touched a rock with the toe of his elk-skin moccasins.

"The cave where they keep the prisoners," Fargo told Logan, "is right at the edge of the hills due east and close to Eagle Rock. He must think they're still alive and maybe they are."

He looked at the contrary warrior again. "*Ipewa.* Good. Where cave white dogs?"

The brave searched memory for an English word. Unable

to find it, he made the motion-of-the-wind sign, then pointed to all three locations again.

"I think," Fargo explained, "that he's telling me they constantly move between them."

The Cheyenne warrior next made the throat-cutting sign, the identifying sign language for the Sioux. Again he pretended to drink, then pointed at Fargo and shook his head violently. He closed one hand and placed it against his forehead, turning it back and forth in that position—the signal of great anger.

"Damn it, I thought it might come to something like this," Fargo said to Logan. "Brennan is enlisting the Sioux to kill us by telling them we're trying to cut off the liquor."

"That danger didn't stop you from cutting off my Tott's Cordial," Logan reminded him. "That, too, could be bad for your longevity. Look, how could this redskin know all that about Brennan and the Sioux?"

"By eavesdropping. Cheyenne can follow much of the Sioux tongue."

Wolf Who Hunts Grinning tired of all this paleface discussion and turned to leave.

"Ha-ho, ha-ho," Fargo called to him, thanking him in Cheyenne.

The stone-faced brave cast another glance at Logan. "Maybe so squaw better," he suggested again to Fargo.

"Fuck you," an irritated Logan retorted.

"Fuck you," the brave retorted like a parrot, liking the sound. He looked at Fargo. "What mean 'fuck you?'"

"Mean same good-bye," Fargo said, unable to think fast enough and on the verge of shooting Logan.

The brave nodded, remembering this.

"Fuck you," he said as he ducked back into the trees.

17

It didn't take Fargo long to realize the Sioux renegades were closing the net on him and Logan.

Around noon the two men reined in at the edge of a meadow to watch the first signals puff up. The thick dark clouds of smoke seemed to squirt into the overcast sky.

"That's coming from within the hills, not out on the plains," Fargo said. "And not that far away."

"What's it say?" Logan asked.

Fargo shook his head. "I can't read smoke and I don't know a white man who can."

"It doesn't have to be about us."

"No," Fargo said, "but I assume it is. The Cheyenne buck just told us how your brother has put Swift Canoe and his renegades on us, and I expected that anyway. But I'd wager this time John is sober, and that's bad for us."

The smoke clouds ceased and soon began to melt away in the wind.

"We're up against it," Fargo said matter-of-factly. "They're going to hunt us the same way they hunt buffalo—squeeze us in from our flanks for the kill."

"How do you know that? You just admitted you can't read smoke signals."

"Does your mother know you're out? The fact that they sent up smoke means they're split into at least two groups and keeping in touch."

"I guess you're the expert," Logan conceded, too sick and tired to much give a damn.

Fargo knew, all right, and he'd rather be hunted down by the cavalry or even the Texas Rangers than vindictive Sioux offended in what they claimed was their tribal birthplace. And it was mighty hard to envision this dying man beside him standing up to an onslaught from arguably the fiercest fighters on the northern plains.

"We'll switch caves," Fargo decided. "That'll shift us away from those signals. Instead of the one at Chinaman's Chance, we'll head for Eagle Rock."

"Isn't that where they're holding the two husbands prisoner?"

"So what?" Fargo said. "Freeing those men ain't the main mile. We do that and then we'd have to break off the hunt and haul them to safety—if there is any to be had. We'll get 'em if and when we can, but first we got bigger fish to fry."

"That 'bigger fish' is all I wanted to hear," Logan said. He stared at Fargo and added: "You never know what might happen when you're working with a 'hero.'"

"Or a back-shooter."

"Precisely, and I'm right behind you."

Fargo stared right back. "I'm safe until you manage to kill your brother. And I won't forget that."

It was Logan who had pushed hardest for a cave-by-cave search over the other options, and Fargo agreed. The Eagle Rock cave held prisoners and, if they were still alive, one of Brennan's thugs would likely show up to check on or feed them. Fargo might then follow the worker bee back to the hive.

But it turned out the Sioux had other plans for them.

By early afternoon the overcast sky had cleared up and white gauze clouds piled up like boulders over the vast plains stretching out to infinity below them. When the wind gusted and nudged the clouds, weird-shaped shadows slid glass smooth along the faded grass. From up in this high clearing Fargo felt like he was looking down on another country in a giant picture book.

But at the moment he wasn't enjoying the scenery—he was confirming a series of mirror flashes from a narrow draw to his right.

"They're in battle mode and soon they're springing their trap," Fargo remarked. "I can tell from their tactics they're stone-cold sober and a helluva lot more dangerous. They're moving in fast now."

"And pissed off about their joy juice," Logan said. "I know how they feel."

"Let's face it," Fargo said. "So far our clover's been deep. But I get nervous when I depend on luck. And christsakes, Brennan, *smother* that damn coughing with your coat. Their hearing is sharp and they know how to use it. Let's get back into the trees."

"Hold up," Logan said as soon as trees surrounded them. "Fargo, I been thinking."

"Better late than never, I guess."

"Seriously. Why do you just automatically trust that Cheyenne? You keep saying how they don't want white men in the Black Hills, so why wouldn't he just set us up for the kill? Your scalp must be worth plenty of wampum."

"It ain't about trust, knothead," Fargo said impatiently. "Hell, I know there's a good chance he might try to kill us after he's had his use of us. Lying to white men is a game. But just because Wolf Who Hunts Grinning deserted his tribe doesn't mean he rejects all the old lore and law-ways."

"In other words, he's not a heretic like me?"

"Hell, I hope not or we're already dead. It doesn't matter that we consider it hokum—to them these hills were once the home of their High Holy Ones. And now those heap big gods have fled because whites searching for the glittering yellow rocks have defiled the place."

Fargo gigged the Ovaro into motion. He had a destination in mind that he hoped wouldn't become a second Chinaman's Chance.

"You mean even the so-called renegades believe all that medicine-gone-bad claptrap?" Logan pressed from behind him.

"I don't s'pose they all do. But plenty of Sioux and Cheyenne think there's a whiteskin invasion."

"And since contrary boy is supposedly under a hoodoo," Logan reasoned aloud, "he can't fight. So he drafts us to fill in—or so it appears. Hell, he could be in cahoots with the renegades. You said the two tribes are cousins."

"Could be," Fargo said cheerfully. "Hell, we were born to die."

"Say, rein in!" Logan called, the effort triggering a coughing spasm.

Fargo cursed and pulled rein, wheeling the Ovaro.

"Speaking of medicine . . . you just said," Logan reminded him, "that my coughing is a threat with the Sioux closing in."

"Skip the parsley and get to the meat," Fargo snapped.

"Didn't you notice how my coughing went way down when I had Tott's?"

Fargo considered the point.

"Even a bad dog is worth a bone," Logan cajoled. "Just one swallow."

"You'll sneak two and you know it. Well, you're useless anyhow."

Fargo dosed him and then led them north. He skirted a suddenly intruded landscape folded into low, stark ridges by ancient glaciers that left heaps of moraine but little screening timber.

"Even I can see this isn't the route to Eagle Rock," Logan remarked, his tone more serene now that Tott's Cordial was ferrying him higher.

"That ship has sailed. What you *can't* see is that we're a few minutes away from a nasty fandango. Never mind that cave; we're fighting to save our dander and I've got another location in mind. Now shut pan and I mean it. They're close now, pinning us down exactly."

As if timed to verify Fargo's experience as an Indian fighter, a shrill, yipping taunt sounded somewhere in the depths of the forested slope.

Logan was impressed and fell silent. The taunt rose again.

Closer, Fargo realized, than he'd thought. If he couldn't reach the spot he had in mind, they'd be forced to flee or fight in dense tree cover. Fargo had survived such battles before, but not with the small number of rifle and handgun cartridges left to him.

As for headlong flight: Fargo could quickly get out onto the plains, but he always tried to avoid outrunning the Sioux at distance on horseback, especially now when the Ovaro hadn't been grained lately.

Another shrill cry on their right, an answering series of sharp yips on their left. Fargo forged on. Just ahead of them the terrain once again changed dramatically and quickly, showing the geologic ravages of some distant upheaval: buttes arose, scree piled at the bases, and the trace Fargo led them along began to corkscrew around natural rock turrets.

Fargo aimed toward a spot above them where a steep slope

of boulders and loose talus and scree formed a funnel. Boulders and slag heaps almost completely blocked any escape from left or right of the slope. A natural rock dike at the top barely held back a jumble of large granite boulders.

Fargo had worked earlier expeditions into the Black Hills as a scout with the U.S. Army Topographical Corps, and he had been present when an army mapmaker labeled this very spot on his map: *unstable landslide slope.*

Rifles suddenly cracked on their right, the Sioux now so close Fargo could hear their mounts snorting. The revenge-thirsting braves sensed victory and their war whoops and piercing cries reverberated through the trees. Some blew shrill eagle-bone whistles, and one must have captured an army bugle someplace: Fargo heard him blowing sour notes to mock the bluecoat pony soldiers.

Logan saw that the two men would soon debouch from the trees and head up steep, cluttered terrain.

"Fargo, the hell are you doing? They'll pick us off like lice!"

"Shut up and listen. They don't know exactly where we are, and from back in the trees they won't see us until they break cover. We need a head start on that slope."

"Look, I don't give a damn about being killed—hell, it would be a favor. But it has to be *after* Cain kills Abel. These savages will kill me on that slope."

"No, they'll kill you if you don't get far enough up it before they spot you. Now chuck the flap-jaw and move on ahead of me through the rest of the tree cover, but *quietly*. Once you break cover, breathe fire into that Arabian. I'm right behind you."

Logan followed orders and moved ahead, wending his way through aspens, spruce and towering ponderosa pine. Fargo took heart when he realized the Sioux warriors were still searching back in the trees, no doubt assuming a savvy warrior like Fargo wouldn't be stupid enough to give up cover.

There was still time, Fargo thought. Time to get up that slope. . . .

Up ahead, Logan had been forced to dismount and lead his high-strung, nervous barb through a narrow defile leading like a roofless hallway from the trees to the rock-strewn slope.

Abruptly, the barb reared up, eyes rolling back in baleful fear until the sockets were nearly all white.

Fargo winced at the horse's high, ear-piercing scream, almost sounding like a female human.

Bear panic. The frontiersman recognized it instantly. The horse had caught a whiff at the wrong damn time.

"I *hope* it was only a whiff," Fargo muttered. There were grizzlies in this area and if one was up ahead, there went any escape up that slope.

Fargo gigged the Ovaro forward even as the random fire behind him became much better focused thanks to Logan's crying horse. The Sioux still hadn't spotted him, but their excellent hearing brought a withering volley of fire in dangerously close around Fargo.

Leaves and bits of stick fell on him as bullets cut in close. Arrows took a long time to fashion and were rarely fired blindly. So if they started whiffing in Fargo would know he was spotted.

"Hold it!" he called ahead to Logan. "Keep its head down and try to cover its eyes!"

But Logan lost the struggle with the panicked barb. It pulled free of the highly weakened man and raced up the slope.

Fargo felt a surge of white-hot anger at Colonel Stanley Durant. Here it was again: the officer had hired a man too weak to hack the job, and Fargo's life was in unnecessary jeopardy because of it. Logan would never make that slope on foot.

Then the first arrow streaked past his face in a bee-humming blur, and Fargo knew he was spotted.

He dismounted in the tight defile and tossed three shots from his Colt to slow their advance before he led the Ovaro through. He practically threw Logan into the saddle and jammed the reins into his hands.

"Take him to the top," Fargo ordered. "Don't try to control his head but keep light pressure on the reins. Hobble him out of sight at the top. How many rounds you got?"

"Twelve in my shell belt, six in my spare wheel, six loaded."

"Be thrifty," Fargo cautioned. "I've got about the same

with the Remington I took from the man I shot in reserve. No shooting just to make noise."

He grabbed the Henry from its boot and slapped the Ovaro hard on the rump. The stallion lowered his hindquarters and laid his ears back flat before launching into motion as if spring-loaded.

Fargo returned to the other end of the defile and rapidly snapped into his favorite make-or-break rifle-firing position, the kneeling offhand. One edge of the defile offered partial protection, but bullets were snapping by so close that Fargo occasionally felt feather tickles from the wind-rip.

Congratulations, genius, he mocked himself as he snugged the rifle butt into his shoulder socket and waited for the advancing braves to form better targets. Here you are, marooned on foot and running low on ammunition while warpath Sioux close for the death hug—and a dying back-shooter escapes on your horse.

Fargo saw a brightly decorated buffalo-hide shield emerge from the trees, then the fierce, copper-skinned warrior carrying it, and he squeezed off his round.

18

Fargo was forced to strict bullet hoarding that severely limited his actions. If he were free to do so, in a life-or-death fray like this one, he would shoot to kill every time and then blaze a streak away from the Black Hills.

But he was a jobber and he had been hired to prevent an all-out Indian war against whites in the volatile Dakota Territory. Killing Sioux, especially in any numbers, right here in the *Paha Sapa* might well ignite that very war.

So Fargo reined in his killing instinct and settled on an unsatisfactory third way for now: he'd try like hell with each bullet to knock a Sioux out of the fight without killing him.

When the first brave emerged from the trees, defiantly dressed in yellow-piped cavalry trousers, Fargo sent a bullet into the meat of his left thigh. A second, a third brave had already bubbled out from the trees. Working the Henry's lever like a demonic machine Fargo shot one in the shinbone, the other in his right forearm.

Counting his handgun loads, which was six bullets expended already, Fargo fretted as he bolted out of the defile and began scrabbling up the slope. Because many of their fellow warriors were blood relatives, the Sioux, like most Indian warriors, were not willing to suffer unnecessary casualties. Fargo hoped they would hold back long enough that he could get a good lead up that slope.

He could see the Ovaro, about halfway up now, Brennan's spooked barb almost at the rock dike. The angle was steep and sometimes Fargo's next step forward, on the unstable slope, sent him two steps backward.

At some stretches Fargo clawed with his hands to assist progress, grasping at small boulders to haul himself up faster.

The fevered din behind him grew loud enough to wake snakes as word of the three wounded warriors fired up the main gather to a kill frenzy.

Now their grievance was even deeper, and Fargo craned his neck as he labored, taking a good look up at that rock dike. He didn't like this desperate idea that was whirling around in his mind half formed. But he had carelessly miscalculated this efficient net Swift Canoe and his renegades had closed around the two whiteskins so quickly—and Fargo figured that desperate situations called for desperate remedies.

The shrill bone whistles, the rusty bugle blasts, the rifle shots, war whoops, yipping taunts—all of it blended into a nerve-jangling racket. Fargo fought his way higher, tearing fingernails, scraping his knees bloody, knowing the Sioux would rush that defile any moment now and discover him crawling upward like a slow, exposed bug.

He watched Logan's unencumbered horse gain the top and slip around one end of the dike. The Ovaro still had about a hundred feet to scale when Spencer and Henry rifles opened up for business behind Fargo.

He tossed a glance over his shoulder. All of a sudden Sioux warriors were popping up like toadstools after a flash flood, drawing beads on him. Fargo took some solace in the fact that most of these northern tribes were still new to marksmanship, some even believing that magic guided bullets, not aiming.

Not so, however, if they nocked their deadly, fire-hardened arrows. Fargo had witnessed up close the skill of Sioux archers, and he felt a cold jolt at the memory.

Fargo had gambled on something else: that the Sioux, like him, were low on cartridges. They were brimming with war excitement and had just wasted precious loads firing blindly at tree limbs. And now the volume of gunfire from below had diminished—Stuart Brennan was a criminal but not a fool. But Fargo believed plenty more bullets were stored somewhere in the hills along with gallons of firewater.

Now and then a round smashed in close to Fargo, and when he sent another glance behind him he saw a brave pulling back his buffalo-sinew bowstring.

Fargo dropped flat only an eyeblink before the arrow whipped over his head and struck a rock in front of him, the flint point spraying sparks before the shaft broke into several pieces from the sudden stopping of its violent force.

The Sioux nocked his next arrow and Fargo cursed, realizing the only way he might save his own bacon and discourage the others from such daring.

The Henry would be too slow to use. Fargo jerked blue steel, pointed more than aimed, hit too high and drilled the Sioux through his throat. Making matters much more gruesome, the brave accidentally staked himself to the slope when he released his bow at the wrong angle and sent the arrow through his own foot. He choked to death on his own blood and the arrow snapped only when he toppled in death.

Damn, Fargo thought, *if these red devils take me alive . . .*

That alarming thought spurred him to a surge of renewed effort, weary arm, leg and back muscles straining and protesting as Fargo played bighorn sheep on the unstable mountain slope, scrabbling faster, higher, fighting off the dizzying waves of exhaustion that washed over him. Now and then, despite the high-altitude chill, he was forced to sleeve sweat out of his eyes.

Scuttling crabwise he threw his left arm out to seize a small boulder for leverage. A rifle barked below, the slug struck a granite boulder well to his left and then "Shit!" Fargo swore when the whining ricochet struck him smack in the funny bone of his left arm, shocking the big nerve that ran close to the surface there.

The blow completely incapacitated his arm at first, leaving it numb, tingling and paralyzed. Fargo saw only surface blood on his elbow, but for at least twenty seconds the pain was so intense he invented new strains of cussing.

The pain subsided quickly to a dull ache, but Fargo's use of the arm returned only gradually. Dragging the useless arm along at first, then able to use it more and more, Fargo continued to scramble for his life.

Again he glanced behind him. Several Sioux renegades were leading strings of ponies up the slope, preparing for a possible chase. The more nimble braves had gained on Fargo before his left arm was functioning. He saw Logan jut into view aiming his Colt Navy to Fargo's left. Fargo glanced that way and saw another Sioux warrior had risen to his feet to launch an arrow at Fargo.

The Navy spat muzzle flame and the Sioux's face turned into a red smear before he toppled backward. Five harrowing minutes later Fargo climbed over the rock dike, sides heaving.

A long, wooded slope spread down the backside of the mountain with open plains beyond it. Logan had both horses hobbled and the moment Fargo arrived he started to knock the hobbles off his barb.

"Hold off," Fargo said, his breathing ragged. "We can't outrun 'em."

"Why not? We've got a lead and good horses. Shit, they're getting closer, Fargo!"

"Our horses aren't rested, and we'd have to break for the plains. Those Sioux mustangs can run from hell to breakfast and back. They don't choke and beat and water-starve their horses to spirit break them, and they'll eventually outrun even my Ovaro. We have to stop them here."

"How? The rest of our ammo might do it, but then what? Or maybe you've got a hat with a rabbit in it?"

Fargo already had his eye on the "how"—a hefty granite boulder teetering like a shaky crown on the edge of the rock dike. But he was in poor fettle and not at all sure he could budge it.

Fargo set his back and shoulders into it, heaving. At his first grunting effort the boulder rocked a few inches, then thumped stubbornly back into place.

"Fargo, never mind playing Samson!" Logan urged. "Those gut-eaters are about to overrun us! Let's hit leather!"

"Hit a . . . cat's tail," Fargo grunted in reply. "C'mon—pitch into the game, calamity howler."

Logan threw his emaciated body against the boulder, but he was barely able to climb into a saddle much less help roll a heavy object. Fargo strained mightily, the muscles in his shoulders and back bunching into thick ropes, and this time the boulder shuddered for a moment as it tried to overcome gravity. But Fargo's tired body gave out and again the boulder *whump*ed back into place.

Fargo took three deep breaths and gave it his best shot.

Again the boulder tipped close to the critical "angle of repose" just beyond which it would whip gravity and roll downward. Fargo strained, failed to roll it, cursed and started to relax his muscles in defeat.

The next moment the Cheyenne contrary warrior materialized at his side, flung Logan aside like a sack of feathers and took his place beside Fargo.

With both men heaving, the boulder rose, popped off the dike, slammed hard into the loose slope and began bouncing down in a stuttering, gathering rumble. The first warning cries went up from the surprised braves.

The slow gathering of noise quickly escalated to a drawn-out explosion. Seen from above, the slope looked like a slow, giant animal shaking itself awake.

Fargo watched a huge dust cloud rise up fast like vented steam, dimming the sun. From below, the Sioux dotting the funnel-shaped slope saw a giant mass of rock and debris bearing down on them, gathering size and speed like a wall of gray water summoned by some angry and malevolent god.

As Fargo had expected, the athletic braves had been able to duck clear on their flanks or flee back into the trees in time. But the front slope was now choked off, and only a long ride around several mountains would put Swift Canoe and his warriors on the back slope.

"Where'd the Cheyenne go?" Fargo asked as he dusted himself off.

"Left without so much as a fuck you," Logan quipped.

"Yeah, it's funny now, but you just better hope he doesn't find out what that really means. Well, I make it two we killed. And I wounded three. They'll be stewing on it for a time. That's why the Cheyenne took off so quick—if the Sioux ever knew he gave us a hand in that tussle, he'd end up watching dogs eat his intestines."

"Piss on the Indians," Logan said while Fargo took a closer look at his elbow. "We've got paler men to kill now. Let's finish that ride to Eagle Rock."

Fargo nodded. Logan seemed buoyed by his latest killing and the prospect of more to come. The grudge light against his brother was back in his eyes now, angrily intensifying the sheen caused by advanced consumption. He lets no man order him around and live, Fargo thought, and that definitely included the order-barking Trailsman.

Fargo said, "These are renegades, but they took losses today and battle death is heap big to them. They'll take time off now to haul the bodies back to the tribe so the squaws can prepare 'em for scaffolds. This might be our best chance to move against your brother. And we'd best not be around when those renegades get done wailing and go back on the scrap."

19

Before the two men escaped off the mountain, Fargo dug out his binoculars and took a quick squint around in the mellow afternoon sunlight.

"I can see the backside of that saddle from here," he remarked. "The one you were shot from."

"I'm touched you remember. Too bad it only wounded me, hey?"

"I can't get all the breaks," Fargo replied.

He focused finer. The body of the ambusher still lay at the bottom of the slope. Wolves or other carrion animals had already eaten one side away, exposing picked-clean ribs. Bluebottle flies covered the dead man's face in a moving mask.

"He should be gone before first freeze," Fargo noted absently.

They wound their way down the slope with no trace to guide them. Fargo halted briefly so the horses could water from a runoff rill. For days now he had felt like he was running hard just to stand still. If he couldn't find and close with those three white troublemakers in a matter of hours, not more wasted days, Fargo feared the council fires would be ablaze with the flames of widespread war.

In truth he feared it was already too late to stop the dangerous mechanism now set in motion.

"Sling your hook, mooncalf," Fargo said when Logan was slow to mount after the horses had watered. "You can die on your own time, not mine."

With visible effort Logan pushed to his feet. "Keep it up, general. The cat sits by the gopher hole."

"That's good," Fargo replied. "Makes for a stationary target."

At least, he reminded himself as he shot an azimuth toward

the plains, the situation at the French Creek camp was a mite improved. Dan Appling had taken Fargo's "suggestion" to heart and cleared out long before sunrise. After Fargo told Jim West why, the word got noised around quickly. Innocent men didn't sneak off like thieves in the night, and every man had quietly counted his gold before breathing easier.

"You like to strut, Fargo," Logan said after he'd mounted. "But you'd be nothing but a pleasant memory in a few females' minds by now if I hadn't saved your ass back on that slope. That red aborigine was about to skewer you."

"Maybe, but so what? You did the job you were paid to do, that's all. But you weren't even doing that. You saved me because you're a dying, soft-handed town man with piss-poor trailcraft—you know you can't find your brother without me. Besides, you want the pleasure of killing me yourself."

"I never said you were stupid."

Fargo no longer bothered to explain plans to Logan. The man was now a one-trick pony, and that one trick was killing his brother and anyone trying to stop him.

Eagle Rock jutted from a slope in the northeastern Black Hills only a quarter mile from the sudden onset of the surrounding plains. Eight miles or so across the open plains rose Bear Butte, which Fargo considered a Sioux sentry outpost for protecting this part of the *Paha Sapa*.

Fargo drew rein on a tree-covered ridge overlooking a dark gray rock shaped vaguely like an eagle's head. He dismounted, muscles aching, and studied the area around the rock carefully through his field glasses.

"I can't pick out the cave entrance," he told Logan, "but you can't miss the little worn-down path Brennan's bunch had made into that thicket just left of the rock."

"All right, so why are we back here with our thumbs up our asses instead of maybe getting something done over there?"

"Settle down, we're on our way. But at the moment there're too few trees and too much light. See those patches of open slope? Sioux and Cheyenne warriors could be anywhere around here, and it's not just the renegades. I want *no* more scrapes with the tribes. I've got that location fixed—we'll go in after sundown. Won't be long."

Fargo couldn't *let* it be long. Especially after that climb up the slope earlier, he felt himself flagging rapidly now. A few hours' sleep would recruit him, but time urgency made him more determined to keep pressing and get this harrowing job over.

Logan, looking more like a dusty ghost than a man, had to slide from the saddle. He sat with his back against a half-rotted log and took out the makings.

"You know, Fargo," he said, trembling fingers spilling tobacco, "holy men dog-ear their Bibles but can't explain men like me."

"I wouldn't waste my time trying. Give me that before you drop it all."

Fargo took the makings from him. He crimped a new paper and shook tobacco into it from a small drawstring sack. He quirled the ends and licked the paper. Fargo repeated the process and handed one to Logan. He struck a lucifer on his tooth and lit both cigarettes.

"Fargo," Logan said after his first inhale triggered a bout of hoarse coughing, "let's have no confusion. The other two are yours, but Stuart Brennan is my assignment."

"I don't care beans about your grudge against your brother. But I don't care who kills him, neither. Just so long as he gets sent under. If you get first crack at him, throw your gun on him. I go for the worst threat first."

Killing Stuart Brennan and his mercenaries was critical, but Fargo had plenty more gnawing at him. There was also ammunition, drugged-up liquor, perhaps more rifles that had to be kept out of the hands of warpath Indians. But instead of strong young troops, Fargo was stuck with a physical wreck for whom mounting a horse had become a near Herculean task—a man who didn't give a damn about the job he was hired for.

The three dirt-workers for the Indian Ring were the biggest threat, and Fargo had to hope the Eagle Rock cave was a key to locking horns with them fast. But getting rid of at least the bullets and liquor was essential, too, and that meant finding them before the renegades did.

For a moment his eyes locked with Logan's, and what Fargo saw brought him within an ace of clearing leather.

Logan laughed so hard he almost shook himself apart coughing. He recovered and gave Fargo a goading grin. "It's getting interesting, isn't it?"

Fargo watched a copper sunset slowly flame out into grainy darkness beyond the hills, turning their outline a deep blue-black.

He almost regretted waiting. The brief rest had let weariness creep in and threaten his alertness. It was time for one of the tricks Dad Bodine had showed him.

Fargo pushed to his feet and dug a plug of chewing tobacco out of a saddlebag and cut off a sliver with his knife. He cheeked it and got it juicing good, then smeared a little of the juice on the inside of each eyelid. The mild but long-lasting stinging thus produced often helped him stay more alert.

"We'll ride as far as that ridge just before the rock, then hoof it," he told Logan. "I don't want our horses near that cave just in case somebody rides up on us."

It turned out Fargo had surmised correctly. Under generous moonlight he easily found the downtrodden grass.

The deeper prints, he quickly determined, were made by loaded pack mules. Might have stored their goods here, he thought—it made sense this close to the plains.

They followed the tracks through a cleverly cutout section of the thicket. In only moments a dark maw yawned before Fargo as he discovered the cave entrance. Very little moonlight penetrated the thicket, and Fargo found it like peering from a dark room into a coal bin.

He pressed against one side of the opening and pushed Logan toward the other.

Fargo listened for several minutes, Logan fidgeting with impatience.

He heard one, no, two voices but not distinctly—just occasional yammering noises that altered slightly with each speaker.

"Hear that?" he called over to Logan.

"Yeah. But who are they?"

Fargo wanted to know that himself, but that cave was darker than the inside of a boot and he'd never been in it before.

"What's the play, Dan'l Boone?" Logan whispered. "I *won't* be blasting my way in here unless Stuart happens to be here. I want my cartridges for the upcoming fraternal reunion."

"Duck back and shut up," Fargo said. "This could open some artillery on us."

Fargo raised his voice. "Myers! Langford! Is that you? It's a friend."

He braced for hot lead but only a startled silence ensued.

"This is Larry Myers," a surprised masculine voice called back. "Who's out there?"

"Skye Fargo and Logan Robinson. You two alone in there?"

"Alone and staked out in irons. If you feel around just inside the entrance you should find a lantern."

While Fargo searched for it, Logan urged him to make this as quick as possible so they could move on.

"We find out what they know, search the place quick for weapons we can use, and move on," he said.

Fargo ignored him as he fired up the wick and turned it higher, holding the lantern out ahead of him. Instead of a narrow cave they were standing in a roomy cavern the size of a double parlor. As he moved the lantern about he spotted a cooking tripod, several crude sleeping pallets made from pine boughs, and two Spencer carbines and a Henry rifle propped against one wall.

"No bribery toys," Fargo muttered, "unless there're other rooms."

"We're right in front of the back wall," called out the second man, who Fargo assumed was Arthur Langford.

"We pump them, and then we leave," Logan reminded Fargo, his bossy tone irritating him.

Fargo's light swept over the unfortunate prisoners, and for a moment sympathy wrenched his belly. The two men were professionally staked out, on a shallow pile of boughs, with prison manacles and chains.

Both young men looked weak and dehydrated and lay in their own filth. But they were alert. Most surprising, to Fargo—they seemed to almost resent his arrival.

"Where's Stuart Brennan?" Logan demanded before Fargo spoke up.

One of the men—Fargo knew it was Larry Myers when he

answered—stared distastefully at the killer. "Does it look like we're privy to his movements? All we know is that he shifts around plenty."

"Does he ever stay here in this cave?" Fargo asked as he gave each man a dipper of water from a wooden pail nearby.

"Twice so far," Arthur Langford answered. "You'll never get these irons off us, Fargo, without the key or a blacksmith. They're top-grade forge-work."

"Any idea where the key is?"

"Some hulking brute named Waco keeps them."

"This Waco can't cuss you out enough, Fargo," Myers added. "He's been madder than a badger in a barrel since you killed his partner, Dobber Ulrick."

"He's also got other things to say about you, Fargo," Langford said. "Including the repeated claim that you were sleeping nights in a very small cabin where our wives stay."

Jesus, Fargo thought. Even criminals gossip. . . .

"What's wrong with that?" he demanded, caught in the act and climbing on his moral high horse to disguise his guilt while he searched for a better approach. "Don't you *want* your wives to be protected?"

"By a man infamous for being a tomcat on the prowl?"

"Well, aren't most men?" Fargo said lamely. "Look, we've got more impor—"

"Wait a minute here," Logan interrupted, enjoying Fargo's suffering. "He's obviously ducking. Look this calico hound in the eyes, gents, and ask him if he screwed your wives. He's guilty as Satan—I *heard* him pour it to that hot little Ursula until she was speaking in tongues."

"Shut your goddamn filthy mouth!" Arthur Langford growled. "You wouldn't get away with talking about my wife that way if you weren't so close to the grave."

"*Ask* him about it," Logan insisted.

Fargo sent him a homicidal glower in lieu of a bullet. Both men stared at Fargo.

"Well?" Myers demanded.

"He's making it up," Fargo lied boldly, meeting their probing stares one at a time and trying to look like his dignity was offended. "Your wives are scared to death for both of you. That's all that's on their minds."

"I was just bullshitting," Logan surrendered. "Damn shame we can't help you two. Let's ride, Fargo."

"Not until I ask a couple more questions," Fargo said. "And quit snapping orders at me. Have you two noticed a routine about their comings and goings?"

"Not much," Myers said. "Except for Waco. He usually comes once a day to feed us, but at different times day and night."

"Has he been here today?"

"No."

"Have they stored guns, ammunition and liquor here?"

"At least twice," Myers said. "We've overheard enough to know they move that stuff around."

"Fargo," Logan said impatiently, "never mind their life story. Let's just—"

"Button it!" Fargo snapped, cocking his head and then turning down the wick. "There's a rider coming in."

20

Fargo heard the faint drumming of hoof-clops cease and then the creak of saddle leather as the rider swung down.

"Nothing happened here," Fargo told the two prisoners tersely. "Logan, get to the left of the entrance—and remember, before you kill him on a whim, that he likely knows where his boss is."

Fargo hurried back to the cave entrance and put the lantern down. He took a few steps back from it and crouched on his heels, Colt drawn.

"Stuart," he heard Logan Brennan whisper to himself as if in fervent prayer. "Let it be Stuart."

A commotion of branches rustling in the thicket grew louder and then boots scuffed to a stop at the entrance.

"Hey, you sorry sacks of shit! Did a bear wander in and eat you? You know, there's a rattlesnake den just down the slope. 'Magine a few of them fuckers comin' in here to hunt, huh? Maybe I'll fetch a few to break up your long, lonely days."

Fargo barely made out his shadow as the new arrival groped around looking for the lantern.

The lantern.

Fargo cursed silently. It would be warm to the touch and warn whoever just arrived.

"Yessiree, Bob," the thug taunted, still feeling for the lantern, "both you boys married to that high-toned pussy and can't even poke it. Yeah, well, guess what: you're both gonna be watching when *I* poke 'em! I'll have them bitches barking like dogs. You—"

A sharp intake of startled breath and Fargo knew the man had felt the lantern's warmth.

A quick scuffling as he retreated back outside the entrance.

"Who the hell's in there?" he demanded. "Somebody lit this lantern not too long ago. Myers! Langford! Sing out now!"

Fargo didn't want to kill him yet. But he didn't see any way out of it now. Just then, however, Larry Myers proved that Adrienne didn't marry a stupid man.

"There's nobody in here now but us," he called out. "But around a half hour ago Skye Fargo was here with that dying killer. He tried to bust our irons but gave up and left. Said he'd be back if he could."

"Left, did he? Are you lying to me, you soft-handed son of a bitch? Is he layin' for me in there, him and that killer?"

"I wish to God he was, Waco," Myers replied in a bitter, hopeless tone. "Then we could have watched him kill you."

This ruse was a stroke of genius that convinced Waco the coast was clear.

"Aww, listen to the bawl-baby," he taunted. "Myers, you're gonna regret them words."

A moment later he struck a match to light the wick. In the sudden flare-up of light Fargo glimpsed a blunt, deeply pock-marked face. It seemed ugly and raw in the red-orange glare.

Lantern light pushed back the darkness as he turned up the wick, and immediately a handgun was cocked on either side of Waco's head.

"Real slowlike," Fargo said, "set the lantern down and pray to God you don't sneeze."

He snatched Waco's Volcanic pistol from the holster and tucked it into his belt. Then he quickly patted the man down for hideout weapons. The hard case had already propped his Spencer carbine against the cave wall to handle the lantern.

Waco complied although with a sneer. "Well, if it ain't buckskin boy and the lunger," he said in a tone caustic as acid. He raised his voice so the prisoners could hear. "Been enjoying that velvet cunny down at French Creek, huh, big hero?"

Logan screwed the muzzle of his Colt Navy into Waco's left temple. "Never mind Fargo. Where's Stuart Brennan?"

"What's it to you, red speckles?"

"I said where is he?"

"Eat shit and die, you little freak. You two are just gonna kill me after I tell you anything, so why the hell would I?"

This man was a bully, all right, but Fargo had learned the hard way that not all bullies were cowards.

Logan's face was a ghastly gray in the flickering light, almost a skull with the eyes sunk deep back in the sockets and the skin stretched tight and parchment thin. The sudden, hard set of Logan's jaw warned Fargo.

"Don't," he told him in a low but firm voice. "Remember who you really want."

He looked at Waco's defiant, belligerent face.

"We know of three caves your bunch is using," Fargo said. "This one, Chinaman's Chance and the one near Blacktail Gulch. Tell us where Brennan is and you're free to light a shuck across the plains."

"Don't blow smoke up my ass, you crusading son of a bitch! After I helped murder your old pal Bodine and kidnapped women you been toppin'? Like hob you'll let me go!"

Waco nodded toward Fargo's Colt. "Tell you what, big hero—they say you're some pumpkins in a dustup. So why'n't you try and *beat* the answer outta me? Give me just *that* much chance"—Waco snapped two fingers—"and I'll knock you into the middle of next week."

Fargo moved farther away and grounded his shell belt, the Arkansas toothpick and Waco's Volcanic handgun. Fargo wasn't up to full fettle, but Waco was the type of insolent loudmouth who made him instantly ache to thrash him.

Waco dropped his gun belt, grinning with anticipation. He was a big, strong man, but Fargo noticed he was also agile and quick on his feet in the manner of men who practiced the European science of fisticuffs.

He stung quickly, wading in fast and catching Fargo with a fast right jab that landed like a brick on his jaw. The blow swung Fargo's head hard to the right and sent him stumbling back a pace or two.

Waco, his ugly, grinning face bright red from sudden exertion, did not let up. Fargo was still reeling backward when the thug landed another solid right, a left, then another right. Each blow landed with a sickening thud, and after these four well-aimed punches Waco stepped back triumphantly, waiting for Fargo to drop.

But after buckling at the knees for a few seconds, the big frontiersman's legs straightened and a game grin found its way onto his bleeding lips.

"Waco, I get the distinct impression you don't much like me."

Waco feinted, then danced inside, easily sidestepping Fargo's wide-arcing swing at him. He jabbed swift and fast, rocking Fargo's head back with each punch.

"Buckskin boy," he taunted, "I'm gonna whip you till your hair falls out."

But the time he wasted goading Fargo was his undoing. Fargo swung from the heels up, all the force of his muscle and will behind a smashing right fist. Droplets of sweat flew from Waco's head. As the man staggered Fargo followed up with a bruising roundhouse left. Waco dropped to his knees and Fargo sent him flat onto his back with a vicious right haymaker.

"Wasting more damn time," Logan complained without a trace of humor.

Fargo, chest heaving, breathing ragged, took a long time to reply.

"Yeah, I agree. I'll drag him across and we'll put him in the manacles. We can make him sing loud." He rummaged in Waco's pockets. "Here, take these and spring the other two."

Logan was reluctant to take the keys. "Damn it, Fargo, you yourself said prisoners would have to wait."

"Well, then, I went soft. It won't matter. I've got a plan that clears them out of here without slowing us down."

Fargo took a few more deep breaths, recovering from his near beat-down. Then he heeled himself and took a groggy Waco by the armpits, beginning to drag his considerable bulk. By the time he reached the back wall of the cavern, both prisoners were practicing walking again.

"That was one humdinger of a fight," Arthur Langford said grudgingly. "He hit more often, but you hit harder."

"This ain't no time to recite our coups," Fargo said. "One of you give me a hand here."

In a minute they had secured Waco's wrists and ankles in one set of manacles. Fargo brought him around with a splash of cool water. The moment he was aware, a sudden squall of rage twisted Waco's lips and tightened his neck muscles into cords.

"All right, blowhard, I whipped you," Fargo said. "Where's Stuart Brennan?"

"Waiting for you to kiss his ass in hell, Fargo! I'm dead, anyway, and I druther eat a handful of maggots than help you."

It wasn't just bravery, Fargo decided. This man was brimful of hatred and spite and just cussed meanness. Now and then he met the type, and too often he had to kill them.

"Gents," Fargo said to Myers and Langford, "maybe you two'd care to step outside for a smoke?"

"If it's all the same to you," Myers said, "we'd rather stay."

"Which cave, Waco?" Fargo demanded.

"Wasting your time, numb-nuts," Waco said. Already his face was lopsided with swelling, his lips so puffy it required effort to force his words past them.

Fargo pressed the muzzle of his Colt hard into Waco's crotch. "Snap out of your tough-boy shit or I'll bullet-geld you here and now. Where's Stuart Brennan?"

Waco's defiance wavered but he didn't crack. Raw hatred wouldn't let him.

"All right," Fargo said. "Just remember that what's coming next is your choice."

Fargo pulled a nail from his possibles bag, then untied his neckerchief.

"Here," he told Logan. "Wrap the head good so you can hold it while you heat the point. Don't stop until it glows red in a match flame."

"What bluff you running now, Fargo?" Waco said with a voice that had lost its swagger.

"Keep it up, curly wolf," Fargo said. "You got no idea in the world what's coming by your own preference. You think your pal screamed hard when I left him gut-shot? Just wait."

Fargo looked at Myers. "Sit on his chest, wouldja? Langford, sit across his thighs after I tug his britches down. We want him real still, and I guarantee you he's going to try to buck hard."

"Hey! Hold up!" Waco protested when Fargo pulled his sailcloth trousers down. "What the hell shit is this?"

"There, there," Fargo said. "You're a tough old soldier, remember?"

"The nail's glowing," Logan reported as he held it out so

Waco could see it. "But let's hurry up. It's burning my fingers through the cloth."

"Just shove it right down his pee hole," Fargo said. "One taste of that and he *will* tell us where Stuart Brennan is—when he can talk again."

"*Jee*-zus, Fargo!" Waco protested, his face a mask of horror. "*Don't!* Brennan and Jack Stubbs are at the Chinaman's Chance cave."

Fargo had to fight back a devious grin. He had never had to actually use the nail in these situations, and in fact was too squeamish to ever do so. But no man, however tough, could withstand even the threat.

"At the cave doing what?"

Waco's fearful eyes fixated on the glowing nail. "Hell, I dunno! Late tonight Brennan has a powwow set up with the Sioux renegade Swift Canoe. The redskin wants more liquor and bullets."

"Yeah, you boys are a sweet outfit, all right. Where's the liquor and ammo?"

Waco hesitated and Logan moved the nail closer to his exposed manhood.

"In the cave with them," he replied hastily.

Fargo looked at Logan. "This is your specialty, Brennan."

"Brennan!" Waco repeated, staring at the wasted, dying man. "Logan Robinson is a Brennan?"

"The entire universe is one big, unsolved mystery," Logan assured him only one second before he sprayed Waco's brains onto the pine boughs.

21

The two former prisoners rode double on Waco's claybank. Fargo led them to a covert about a mile from Eagle Rock.

"Here's Waco's carbine," Fargo said, handing it to Myers.

"Fargo, we need those damn weapons," Logan protested.

"Come down off your hind legs. I'm giving you Waco's pistol and reloads. The way you shoot, you'll have enough rounds."

"But how long will we be here?" Myers complained. "We haven't seen our wives in—"

"We all got our troubles," Fargo cut him off. "If I'm not back in a day I'll likely be dead or dying. In that case you two head due south from here for three-quarters of a mile. You'll hit Middle Creek, not much more than a trickle stream. Turn right and follow it until it feeds into a second, bigger creek— that's French Creek. Follow it upstream until you reach the prospectors' camp. It's the long way but you'd need a map to follow the short route."

Fargo tossed down two blankets and a sack of pemmican he'd taken from the cave.

"Lie low in that covert, gents, and keep your voices down. Gather up pine needles for the horse. Keep him tethered close but give him enough line to walk around a little. The Sioux around here are wound up to a fare-thee-well, and they'll roast your brains if they find you. If you have to strike out on your own, I recommend traveling after dark."

Fargo handed the Volcanic, a small-bore repeater less reliable than a Colt, and the extra shells to Logan. The two men gigged their horses north toward the cave near Chinaman's Chance.

"I hope we catch them before they leave to meet with the

Sioux," Logan fretted. "They might not even return to the same cave."

"That bothers me, too," Fargo said. "But I'd wager there is a parley set for tonight like Waco said. But your brother is already short one man. That means he and Jack Stubbs should be waiting for Waco to return before they ride out to face red John."

"Yeah, that rings right. And when he doesn't show up they'll know there's trouble. So they'll fort up with enough loaded repeating rifles to outgun a cavalry regiment."

"That's how I make it," Fargo said. "And we're better off now but we still don't have the ammunition for a long bullet swap."

"You're an old hand at poker," Logan said. "You know you have to risk big to win big."

"Know it? Hell, it's my anthem. But we're not just running into the cave with guns blazing—they could shoot us to doll rags."

"You're the expert on that. But, Fargo, however we play it, Stuart is *mine*."

"Then you'd better throw down on him fast, Mad Dog, because I never use place cards. I always try to shoot the most dangerous threat first."

"Then we know where we stand. *I'm* killing Stuart and you'd be wise to accept that. You'll have enough trouble with Jack Stubbs."

"Then throw down on your brother fast," Fargo repeated. "But from everything you've said about him, seems to me you're painting him as too much of an easy kill. You figure him to just roll over because you're pissed at him?"

"No," Logan admitted, his tone sobering now. "Tell you the truth, Fargo, I rate our chances less than even. Even when we were kids I never once bested that son of a bitch. Nobody could. But I'm going to try my damnedest to turn his toes up."

They rode in silence for perhaps half an hour, each man alone with his thoughts, Fargo listening intently to the night. The insect rhythm was strong and steady, which Fargo read as a good sign, and a wolf howled from a ridge or two over. But Fargo's distance-trained hearing picked up another faint sound borne on wind gusts: the nonstop *siss*ing of water.

Fargo led on through a dense forest that forced the Ovaro to a walk. Low branches were a constant hazard and sometimes both men had to fold low over their pommels to get through. Finally they broke out into a clearing and Fargo saw it out ahead: a silver-white reflection where moonlight bathed the large, high cataract's shimmering curtain of water.

"I scouted that area when the army mapped it," Fargo said. "But mostly I was looking for Indians. That Cheyenne buck definitely said 'cave water.' I've found them before behind waterfalls."

Logan pulled his coat up over his mouth to smother the sound of coughing. Fargo swung down to check his cinches and latigos and the action of his weapons.

"Fargo," Brennan said when he recovered, "Stuart isn't the type to make a last stand in a confined area like a cave—unless there's another way out. When we were shirttail brats, even, he kept the bedroom window open in the dead of winter he was so afraid of being trapped. He hated rooms with only one door and never used an outhouse—even when it was zero degrees outside, he tramped out into the woods to do his business. All this started after he saw our mother's coffin sealed and her body lowered into the ground. My great fear is that he'll melt away the moment he feels the danger of being trapped is too great."

"All that's good to know," Fargo said, "but hard to stop. It's just another reason to play this thing smart, and then strike fast so he doesn't have time to vanish."

"Jesus," Logan said in an almost desperate voice, only now thinking of it, "they could simply have pulled out by now."

"That's why we have to get closer and get a better size-up. C'mon."

"Hold on a minute," Logan said.

The Trailsman couldn't believe his ears.

"Don't tell me you're getting ice in your boots," he said.

"It's just a quick item of business. Fargo, at one time I hoped to get back to Fort Pierre. That was wishful thinking and I know now that I won't."

"Christsakes," Fargo whispered impatiently, "this is no time to dwell on your damn regrets."

"Listen! If you survive this job would you be interested in

another? Only this time a featherbed job that pays four hundred dollars in advance?"

"That's a sight of money, all right," Fargo agreed, some of the impatience seeping from his tone as curiosity replaced it. "Who's hiring me?"

"I am. You'll find four hundred in gold cartwheels—twenty double eagles—wrapped up in rawhide at the bottom of my nearside saddlebag."

"And you claimed back at Fort Pierre you took this job because you were flat busted."

"Imagine that," Logan retorted sarcastically. "A cold-blooded murderer who also tells lies."

"I walked right into that one," Fargo admitted. "But what's the deal on this job?"

"There's a letter of instruction with the gold. Basically it's just body-escort duty. My body, of course."

"I thought your big idea is to kill me after you pop your brother over? How can I escort you anywhere if I'm dead?"

"That was my big idea until I realized you could render me this great—and highly profitable for you—last service."

"And knowing you planned to murder me, why wouldn't I just take the gold and leave you for the worms?"

Logan snorted. "Because you're one of those disgusting idiots with a 'code.' That's why I hate you, Fargo. No real man curbs his natural impulses to obey some rules set up by psalm-singers. You'll fuck married women and lie to their husbands about it, sure. You're a bachelor, a hound who follows no god, and you figure nobody misses a slice off a cut loaf. But if you hire on for a job, you'll do it come hell or high water even if your employer dies and you've got the money."

"Well, neither one of us is dead yet," Fargo said dismissively. He kicked the stirrup straight and stepped into it. "Right now we work on staying alive and killing our enemies, not burial details. Let's rustle."

The clock had been set ticking when Stuart Brennan arrived in the Black Hills, and Fargo knew, as the horses picked their way closer to the cataract, that an Indian-paleface war could erupt any day now.

Only something that urgent, and knowledge of what such

wars produce, could have kept him on the job. But Fargo was an unlikely martyr. Unlike the dying Logan Brennan, Fargo greatly valued his own life and he didn't want to be anywhere near these hills when those Sioux renegades finished mourning their dead and crossed their lances against Skye Fargo.

It had come down to this time and place *if* those two imported jackals were indeed in that cave. Fargo knew Waco was a defiant, hateful son of a bitch. Any answer he gave Fargo in that Eagle Rock cave would have to be believed, and Waco knew it.

They had circled around to a long ridge just above the wide curtain of misting spray. Fargo hauled back on the reins and dismounted, leading the Ovaro behind a tangle of ferns and saplings and tethering him short. Logan followed him, his fluid-filled lungs bubbling audibly and forcing him to take rapid and shallow breaths.

"I wonder where they keep their horses?" Logan said in a voice just above a whisper. "If there is another way out of that cave, it would be useless without horses."

Fargo pulled the captured, black-gripped Remington from a saddlebag and stuck it behind his shell belt before he pocketed the dozen reloads for it. He left his Henry in its scabbard.

"I'm gonna look around for those mounts," he told Logan. "Wait here with the horses and keep your short iron to hand. My rifle's here if you need it."

Fargo fanned out in fast, concentric lines, the experienced scout systematically searching the tree-choked slope with its thick tangles of brush. Twenty minutes later he discovered the horses and pack mules in an exceptionally well-hidden rope corral.

Three of the horses stood saddled. Ready, Fargo surmised, for an escape by Brennan and Stubbs if a fight went bad for them. But why a third horse saddled? He quickly searched all the saddlebags but found no weapons.

Fargo stripped the leather from one horse and had just started in on a second when a twig snapped somewhere behind him.

Fargo pulled steel and tucked at the knees, heart suddenly pulsing in his ears. Twigs didn't break themselves and he never ignored the sound.

It could be Logan, he thought, champing at the bit to kill his brother and impatiently breaking orders to hurry Fargo along.

Or it could be Sioux closing in on him. Nor could he rule out Brennan and Stubbs using their horses as a lure.

Fargo waited for uncounted minutes, listening. He heard nothing else and finished stripping the second and third mounts. He used his Arkansas toothpick to slice through a rope and drove the animals off by whipping them with his hat.

"Christ!" Logan swore when Fargo returned. "Still with the Daniel Boone shit?"

"Daniel Boone just drove off their horses, chucklehead. Settle down and follow me. You'll have to do some climbing, and I'm damned if I'm helping you."

Fargo moved to the sudden drop-off in the ridge that had created the cataract from great amounts of runoff water on the higher slopes. He backed over the lip and scrambled down using rocks and roots as handholds. A brief descent brought him to a limestone shelf about ten feet wide, its farthest edge in the streaming water. Cold mist enveloped Fargo and made him shiver.

Logan made it down and moved up behind him. All was dark ahead of them between the falling, moon-shimmering water on their left and the stone face of the cliff wall they were now hugging on their right.

"Wait here," Fargo whispered above the hissing water. "I've got to locate that cave."

"Fargo, don't you—"

"Why don't you set that shit to a tune? I'm *not* going for kills yet," Fargo cut him off impatiently. "Just a reconnoiter. You'll be hammering caps with me when we open the ball. With luck I'll even be able to spot your brother for you so you can get that first kill."

"That must be why you didn't even ask me what he looks like."

"Don't worry. I'll know him."

Fargo had been caught lying through his teeth. If he got the chance to drop both men by himself he'd do so and then afterward shoot it out with an enraged Logan. But criminals, he'd discovered long ago, seldom catered to his desires during showdowns. Whatever ultimately happened here would fit no plan and would be decided in an instant's thought and action.

The readiness was all.

Fargo inched along the limestone shelf, his Colt filling his right hand. He pressed as tightly as he could against the stone face behind him to minimize his profile in case someone peered out from a cave.

If there was even one here, he reminded himself. He was relying on shaky translations from a contrary warrior whose English vocabulary was mostly limited to some variation of "maybe so better not."

Fargo was halfway across the width of the falls, soaked by now and starting to believe the Cheyenne meant *near* the waterfall, not behind it.

He slid along for three more feet and thought he saw dim light ahead—and heard a voice droning. Suddenly he flinched when a glowing cigarette butt landed a few feet ahead of him. Moments later Fargo just made out a rifle barrel emerging into view.

His thumb cradled the hammer of his Colt and Fargo's mind went calm as his muscles coiled for action.

22

"No need to assume the worst yet, Jack," Stuart Brennan told his topkick. "Waco is late but that hardly proves he's dead. And if we are in imminent danger as you believe, constantly sticking your head outside of the cave is hardly prudent."

"Yeah," Stubbs agreed, backing away from the entrance. "But it wasn't hardly more than a day ago that Fargo bucked Dobber out in smoke. And look how he gave Swift Canoe and the rest of them blanket asses the slip. Besides, he knows *every*thing—even the deal with the bitches at French Creek. Fargo and Robinson are on us close and they mean to free our souls."

"I told all three of you repeatedly that Fargo is chain lightning. But we have no reason to believe he knows about this or any of our caves. If we do end up being attacked here, Jack, we're not making any foolish 'stand'—not against those two. We get out quickly to the horses and build a lead."

"Boss," Stubbs said, "you know me—I'm with you till the wheels fall off. But it's no good. We're down to bedrock and showing damn little color. I say we just leave the tornado juice and the cartridges right here and bust loose from these hills before Fargo or the Sioux kills us."

"We'll be busting loose, all right," Brennan said. "But if we pull foot now we're tossing thousands of dollars right down a rat hole. Swift Canoe and his braves want that Indian burner like the damned want ice water in hell. Right now it seems like magic to them, big medicine, power. The strychnine addles their thinking."

"But you yourself said they'll wise up as soon as it stops being new to them and they figure out how it ain't medicine."

Brennan dismissed this with a negligent wave. "That's one

of the risks we take. But I think this next attack on French Creek, on top of the massacre at Spearfish Creek two days ago, should give our employers all the ethnic friction they seek. Absent an all-out war, however, I'm reimbursed only for the supply outlays."

The two men sat on upended cartridge boxes, a "dark lantern" burning low between them. Its sliding panels blocked most of the light from beaming toward the entrance. For a moment sudden anger at Fargo made Brennan's eyebrows arch and his thin-lipped mouth set itself hard. His eyes looked like molten metal.

"If it wasn't for Fargo," he muttered his thought aloud, "Logan could never have found me."

"How's that, Mr. Brennan?"

Fargo, listening to all this just outside the cave, never heard Brennan's next remark—something bowled into him from behind and sent him sprawling loudly in front of the entrance, the Henry clattering hard.

He heard Logan's Colt Navy open up right behind him and almost immediately the crackling rat-a-tat of handgun and rifle fire answering from the cave, the sounds greatly amplified by the close stone walls and banging on Fargo's eardrums.

Logan, that half-crazy son of a bitch! The Henry had skidded out of Fargo's reach. He rolled onto his left hip and opened up with his Colt, aiming at the seemingly endless muzzle flashes.

He heard a harsh grunt when Logan was struck and fell to his knees, but the dying killer kept squeezing off rounds, emptying his wheel, knocking it out, loading his spare. Fargo saw this only in fractional glimpses because the shooter on the left had spotted Fargo's muzzle streaks and opened up on him with a vengeance.

He recognized the sound of a Henry cracking at him. Slugs chewed into the limestone shelf only inches from Fargo. Inside the cave there was a strangled cry of pain before the gun on the right fell silent. But Fargo and the second man continued to chuck lead at each other, locked in the deadly dance.

Fargo's hammer clicked on an empty shell casing. There was no time to fiddle with his spare cylinder. He dropped the Colt and jerked the Remington from his belt.

The gun jumped in Fargo's hand, jumped again, but the Henry's magazine just kept feeding lead. Fargo felt a quick, hot lick of pain when a round grazed his thigh. The hammering racket inside the cave reverberated like the trumpets at Jericho and seemed to build louder and louder as Fargo fired his third, his fourth rounds from the Remington.

Still the Henry peppered him as Fargo fired a fifth time. A moment later the shooting just ceased like a door shutting. The Henry clattered to the floor followed by a heavier *flump* as a body followed it.

This sudden, peaceful silence after the chaos and din of the intense cartridge session seemed unreal to Fargo, whose ears were still ringing. The acrid, sulfurous stench of spent powder stained the air. Fargo smelled the familiar, sheared-metal odor of copious amounts of fresh blood.

He pushed to his feet, stepped past Logan's still form, and opened the panels on the dark lantern. Crates of ammunition were stacked against one wall, cases of liquor another.

It was easy to tell by facial resemblance which of the two dead men was Stuart Brennan. He had been shot once through the heart. The man who must have been Jack Stubbs showed three bullet holes, including one through the liver.

Again that thought picked at Fargo like a burr: *why a third saddled horse?*

Fargo carried the lantern back toward Logan Brennan, expecting to find a corpse. But the notorious assassin, despite two bullets in his lungs and a shattered knee, was somehow clinging to life.

"Is he, Fargo?"

"Dead as they come. You bored him right through the heart, Mad Dog. I got Stubbs in the nick of time, too. It's an even split: we each dropped two."

Logan was desperately trying to swallow air, and pink foam bubbled on his lips.

"Yeah, I kill 'em, don't I?" he managed. "Fargo, I don't like you and I never did. At first I . . . I really did intend . . . intend to kill you after I got Stuart."

"I figured that out early on. I intended to shoot you first."

"But you will take . . . take the job I offered?"

"For the four hundred dollars, yeah. Not as a favor to a murderer like you."

"Yes, Reverend Fargo. If you hurry maybe you can . . . can baptize me. . . . *Christ*, that hurts!"

Logan nearly doubled up as pain jolted through him hard. "I can't see anything, Fargo; did the lantern go out? It's here, isn't it? I'm crossing over."

"It's best this way," Fargo said, cocking the Remington. He'd seen this before, and the pain would now rapidly get worse.

"Ma?" Logan said, his body twitching in rapid seizures. "Ma, is that fresh bread I smell?"

"It's on that plate to your right," Fargo said.

The dying Logan, his face twisted with fiery pain, turned his head in that direction and Fargo shot him just above the left ear.

He should have danced a strangulation jig long ago, Fargo thought, looking at the ashen-faced, wasted-away form lying half inside the cave, half outside on the shelf. But he had turned out to be one tough son of a bitch who wouldn't be denied his prey. Already near death from consumption when this ordeal started ten days ago, he absorbed four bullets and plenty of hardships before he finally pegged out.

Fargo stuck the empty Remington back in his belt and picked up Stubbs' Henry, glancing at the empty breech. He worked the lever but the magazine, too, was empty.

"Shuck the artillery, Fargo."

Dan Appling, his jaundiced skin like old parchment in the lantern light, stepped into view from behind the stack of liquor cases. His revolving-cylinder Colt rifle was aimed plumb center on Fargo.

"*Drop* that rifle, I said. Don't get cute on me, Fargo—I'm hair-trigger."

Fargo dropped the Henry, not liking the homicidal glint in Appling's stare. Fargo had known all along that somehow that third horse meant trouble.

"Thought I ran, huh, pretty boy? Thought you scared me shitless. Well, thanks to you Brennan had a job opening. He was smart to keep me hid."

"Smart? Hell, he's dead. I'd say Brennan was hog stupid to rely on you. You never even got into the fight."

"What, with all that hot lead ricocheting everywhere? I ain't stupid like you and the lunger. Now all I gotta do is douse your glims and pocket that four hundred dollars the lunger just mentioned."

Fargo saw his finger slip inside the trigger guard and felt his back go clammy with cold sweat. *Tuck and roll,* his mind told him, *but time it perfect and get him on the ground.*

"Yeah," Appling said, his voice tight with hatred, "you're the big man, Fargo. You told me back at camp that if I threatened you one more time I'd be sucking wind through a bullet hole. But you're the one who—"

The arrow that suddenly rocketed through the entrance of the cave and pierced Appling's side was painted lake blue and fletched with crow feathers. He shrieked and staggered backward, but a very nervous Fargo saw the rifle was still aimed at his lights.

Both Fargo's handguns were empty and his long gun still lying outside. But the Trailsman had a name for an empty rifle close to hand: it was called a war club.

While Appling still stood, wide-eyed with shock and staring at the arrow, Fargo scooped up Stubbs' empty Henry and bashed in Appling's skull with the stock.

Fargo glanced at the Cheyenne arrow, its flint point dripping gore, and felt a grin easing his lips apart as he recalled that twig snapping earlier.

Wolf Who Hunts Grinning had secretly assisted only three times: just now, a day earlier when he helped Fargo stop the attacking Sioux with a rockslide, and when he told Fargo where the three caves were located. But the contrary warrior had been instrumental in this important victory over Stuart Brennan.

Fargo made a quick study of the cave, and about fifteen feet beyond the point where Stuart Brennan lay dead he found a big cleft in the wall. Cold air blew briskly into his face, and Fargo knew this was the second way out that Logan had sworn his brother must have. Logan's great fear of his brother escaping had forced tonight's close-quarter shoot-out before Stuart could even react.

There was one rather pleasant task that remained, and despite his bone-weariness Fargo tied into it gladly.

He used his toothpick to pry the tops off the cases of liquor bottles packed in excelsior. He pitched each bottle back into the cave, shattering them on impact. The cartridges he dumped into the deep pool at the bottom of the high cataract after pulling out a generous supply of Henry ammunition for himself.

By the time Fargo finished he could barely keep his eyes open. He glanced around at the four bodies.

"Well, at least there won't be a problem with any of them snoring," he reasoned.

Fargo curled up on the cave floor, using his arm for a pillow, and in less than thirty seconds fell sound asleep among the dead men.

23

"You don't look too comfortable," Fargo remarked, trying to keep a straight face at the sight of Adrienne, all togged out in her finery, clinging precariously to the back of an ugly, squealing mule.

When she turned her head to look at Fargo in the sunlight, golden specks flashed to life in her irises. Man, she's easy on the eyes, Fargo thought.

"Yes, it's rather trying," she admitted. "My clothing constantly requires 'a good tug-down' as my aunt Martha used to say."

"There's more than enough to tug down," Fargo assured her, again trying not to laugh outright. "You're dressed mighty fancy to be sailing on a mule."

Adrienne did look striking in a full skirt with a small waist, scallop-flounced, and a cloak with a sealskin collar. She carried a swansdown muff, now tucked behind her cloak, and her hands seemed dainty in apple-blossom pink gloves.

"Would you prefer that we dress in bloody buckskins like you do?" Ursula teased him from the back of a second mule. "And boots with big, terrible knives tucked into them?"

"You two could turn heads if you wore scrub rags," insisted Jim West, who rode with a group of five other prospectors from the now deserted French Creek camp.

The party of eleven riders bore due east across brown, rolling plains toward Fort Pierre, the Black Hills a bad memory well behind them now. Larry Myers rode Waco's claybank, Langford one of the mules they had purchased at the trading post near Last Stand Gulch.

Both husbands kept a wary eye on Fargo when he rode near

their wives. But they recognized a debt and remained civil to the man who rescued them from certain death and then brought them back to French Creek to reunite with their wives. Once they had told their story to the prospectors, emphasizing how Stuart Brennan had stirred up the explosive anger of the Sioux, the sourdoughs had voted to pull up stakes before red death swept over them.

Fargo welcomed the decision by six of them to ride to Fort Pierre. They were well armed as were Myers and Langford. But even more he welcomed the decision by both husbands to keep their business back in the States. The American West was still no place for people who used tablecloths.

"Do you think the death of Stuart Brennan," Myers asked Fargo, "and your destruction of their liquor and munitions will pacify the Sioux?"

"Pacify? The Sioux will never become cracker-and-molasses Indians," Fargo replied. "They're horse warriors and fighting is in their blood. When they aren't actually at war, they're practicing war. And the white man won't stop taking over the ranges they claim. So the worst is yet to come. All me and Logan did was shore up the ruins a little."

"And save plenty of lives in the process," Adrienne added. "Ours included. Skye Fargo, you are a brave gentleman."

Her tone of obvious admiration caused Myers to clear his throat. Fargo couldn't blame him for his jealousy and had remained carefully circumspect with both women. They, however, were pampering and praising him much to their husbands' chagrin.

"I'm not certain you got all of that liquor, Fargo," Langford spoke up. "That one brave who accosted us yesterday *had* to be snockered."

A grin pulled at Fargo's lips. The party had just emerged from the Black Hills near the Cheyenne River when Wolf Who Hunts Grinning had appeared atop a ridge. With the full force of his lungs, he had hollered, "Fuck you!" at the departing whiteskins as he held his shield aloft.

"That was just a little mix-up with translation," Fargo assured him. "More of Logan Brennan's tomfoolery although I had a hand in it, too."

"It's very eerie," Ursula chimed in, "to know Logan's body is traveling with us. You wouldn't think a man who lived as he did would be so preoccupied with the fate of his remains."

Fargo agreed. But he was being paid well to carry out the instructions in Logan's letter. For fifteen dollars the body had been sewn tight into a canvas sheet at the trading post after packing it with quicklime to preserve the remains.

It was now secured to Logan's coal black barb, following Fargo on a lead line. At Fort Pierre Fargo was to ship the body by Overland Express, accompanying the freight wagon every foot of the way to a little town called Maryville in northwest Missouri. A detailed map showed Fargo the exact meadow where he was to bury the body himself without a coffin and in an unmarked grave.

"What's the mystery behind all of it, Skye?" Adrienne asked him.

"Lady, that man's mouth was a mill run. But he never even uttered a peep about it to me, and I don't push into a man's past—especially a man I don't like."

"Rugged and tough, aren't you?" Ursula teased.

Fargo removed his hat and placed it over his heart. "That's a libel on me. I'm a lovable cuss."

This time both husbands cleared their throats simultaneously, and Fargo figured it must have been his careless choice of the word "lovable."

"Skye, the U.S. Army is still trapped between the sap and the bark," Colonel Stanley Durant said. "That infernal Indian Ring will never give up while there's so much federal money to skim off. But your efforts have purchased valuable time, and one can always hope some of these new 'reformers' are not just more profiteers. Thanks for your good work."

"Yeah," Fargo said in a flat tone, watching Durant closely across the commander's vast and immaculately neat desk. "My 'good work' would've been one helluva lot easier to take if you hadn't stuck me in the traces with a dying assassin. You got any idea what it feels like to know the man *behind* you is a notorious back-shooter?"

Durant only partially suppressed a grin. Unlike the unsure, despondent Colonel Durant of two weeks earlier, this one once again showed the quick, deliberate movements of energetic men who get a day's work done by noon.

"You admitted he saved your life and killed two of the four agents," Durant pointed out. "One of them being the kingpin—his brother."

"He did a good job there. And he *might* have saved my life—that Sioux arrow could have missed me. And the second white man that he killed was staked down—hell, a monkey can pull a trigger."

Fargo leaned forward in his chair.

"Colonel, that man's poor health and sick, criminal brain put me at unnecessary risk. All right, he did a good job, taken by and large. But I had to watch him like a hawk because he was a snap killer who resented orders. You had to know that. It ain't like a careful military man to take that chance."

"You didn't warm up to him at all?" Durant probed.

"No point turning dung into strawberries, is there?"

Durant nodded. "I'd be disappointed in you if you didn't feel that way. His brand of evil comes straight from hell. An Apache wouldn't waste a bullet on him—he'd kill him with a rock. But he wasn't always that way, Fargo."

"Hell, every man once sucked at the teat, Colonel. By the time I met him he was a dangerous, low-down, murdering son of a bitch."

"Fargo, I want to tell you something. But it can't leave this office, right? Some of it was confided to me by a lady."

Fargo nodded, curious to hear more.

"Our fort provost martial is Captain Leland Bursons, a fine young officer. His wife, Clarissa, has become our unofficial post sweetheart. But long before she was married, when she was a girl of fifteen, she lived in Maryville, Missouri."

Fargo's interest deepened.

"She was courted briefly by Logan Brennan," the colonel continued. "He was eighteen then, and like many young lads in that wild area he was known for being harum-scarum—an occasional troublemaker but *not* a killer. That came later."

"When I saw him on the bluffs over the fort," Fargo said, "I wondered if there was a woman in the mix. This meadow where I'm burying him—it's where he met Clarissa?"

"Yes. His very name is gall and wormwood to her now. But

back then she had fallen in love with him—if a fifteen-year-old can properly be said to be in love. There was one ominous fly in the ointment: Logan's brother, Stuart, wanted the same girl, but she rejected him for Logan."

"I can finish the sketch," Fargo said. "This killing grudge Logan carried toward his brother: it was because Stuart raped her?"

"And savagely beat her. He was never seen in the area again. And to spare her reputation, the crime was never reported."

Fargo watched Durant pull a handkerchief out of the inside pocket of his tunic and wipe the glistening sweat from his forehead.

"Colonel," he said, "years ago didn't you use to be in charge of an army supply depot in northwest Missouri?"

Durant gave a curt nod. "I was a major then. It was very close to Maryville, and my family was with me."

"I've never met her," Fargo said, "but I know you have a married daughter. Seems I heard you mention the name Carrie."

Durant gave another curt nod. "Yes. My wife constantly harangues me—tells me it's an 'improper diminutive' for a girl named Clarissa."

Fargo sat silent for about ten seconds. A dozen questions had just been answered to his satisfaction. Any others would go unasked. He stood and clapped on his hat.

"It was a worthy mission, Colonel," he said, extending his hand, "and I got no complaints. Glad I could help—and to know Logan had one decent thing in him."

A sly grin crept onto Durant's normally stern lips. "Always mystify, mislead and surprise. I learned that from a reprobate named Skye Fargo."

"I know the man," Fargo said as he headed toward the door. "Good-looking cuss and a favorite of the ladies. But quite often he's full of shit."

"Where you headed?" Durant asked his retreating back.

"After I plant Logan's body, I figure I'm way overdue for a loafing spell."

"Well, once the whores have all your money, I can always find work for you here at Fort Pierre."

"There're easier ways to get myself killed," Fargo shot back before swinging the door shut.

Outside, the air was crisp and the morning sunshine so brilliant it made him sneeze. He watched a squad of soldiers drilling and reminded himself: life on the frontier was hard, all right. Death was as real as a man beside you, a man who never went away.

Fargo accepted that and even thrived on it. It was one plague after another of smallpox or yellow fever or cholera, with Indian raids a constant threat. And even when a host of mortal enemies didn't lurk, an unending series of flash floods, landslides, twisters and wild animal attacks was unavoidable.

For those very reasons, Fargo had decided long ago, a man had to drink life to the lees and live it full-bore while he still had breath in his nostrils.

The next fight was coming as surely as sunrise in the morning, and just as surely Fargo would be ready for it—even eager.

LOOKING FORWARD!
The following is the opening
section of the next novel in the exciting
Trailsman series from Signet:

TRAILSMAN #396
DEAD MAN'S JOURNEY

*Mojave Desert, California, 1858—where it's
open season on Skye Fargo in a hellish landscape
littered with bleached bones.*

"It's the work of the Scorpion," Fargo announced with grim confidence, unfolding to his full six feet and slapping the sand and grit from the knees of his buckskin trousers. "That throat cut, exactly like a surgeon's work from one earlobe to the other, is his trademark. I hear it's how he announces his presence to his victims."

A Mexican stock tender Fargo knew only as Lupe lay sprawled on his back in a dry creek wash where scores of boulders were heaped, his tongue swollen so thick it protruded like a leather bladder. Red ants in a feeding frenzy had already eaten the eyeballs down to the bone sockets.

"God dawg! Who's the Scorpion?" asked an army private so young he looked like a mascot.

"Pablo Alvarez," replied the second man with Fargo, Stanton "Grizz Bear" Ormsby. "Quicksand would spit that son of a buck back up. This here is all we lacked—thank you, Jesus."

Fargo sent a careful glance all around them, then focused his sun-slitted, lake-blue eyes to the middle distances and expanded his search, sweep-scanning the harsh landscape. His scalp had prickled the moment he recognized the bloody calling card of the Scorpion.

Excerpt from **DEAD MAN'S JOURNEY**

Unrelenting sun and dry wind had cracked his lips. The almost unbreathable air felt brittle with warmth that seemed to radiate from a giant furnace. All around them, as far as the eye dared to look, the arid brown folds of the Mojave Desert stretched on unbroken, ending in a shimmering heat haze on the far horizon. Barely visible in the rippling blur due west was a line of dead black mountains—a reminder of the daunting conditions awaiting any fools who challenged Zeb Pike's Great American Desert.

Only ten minutes after sunrise the morning mist had burned off the nearby Colorado River. When Lupe didn't turn up for breakfast, Fargo, Grizz Bear and Private Jude Hollander—proud, razor-nicked member of the U.S. Army Camel Corps' fifteen-man security detail—rode out to look for him. The circling buzzards were like an aerial fingerboard pointing to his nearly decapitated corpse.

"Shit, piss and corruption!" Grizz Bear exploded. "Ain't enough of a holiday, is it, how we spent the last three weeks huggin' with them Skeleton Canyon Apaches. Now we got warpath Mojaves out front of us and this murderin' greaser Alvarez deals himself into the game. Hell, who *wouldn't* work for the army?"

"You bawl too damn much," Fargo admonished the veteran frontiersman. He nodded toward Private Hollander. "You never hear soldier blue pissing and moaning like a weak sister."

"Soldier? *This* pee doodle?" Grizz Bear snorted, dry sand popping out of his nostrils. "Hell's fire! He's a fuzz-faced brat in ready-to-wear boots. You know, Fargo? This tad woulda give the apple *back* to Eve."

"Who's Pablo Alvarez?" Jude Hollander asked again, well used to Grizz Bear's roweling. "He got one of them road gangs like that bunch we chased off a few days back?"

Fargo was slow to answer, still focusing his attention on the surrounding terrain, habitually thinking like potential enemies and deciding where he'd hole up for an ambush attempt. The dead stock tender might also be a lure for distracted fools. . . .

Fargo's hair-trigger alertness had been challenged, but not dulled, by weeks of grueling and dangerous travel across West

Texas and the New Mexico Territory, fighting Comanches and Kiowas, Apaches, two roving gangs—and some of the foulest, most difficult, heartiest and most bizarre beasts of burden the U.S. Army ever sent on a supply mission.

"You can chuck that road-gang talk," Fargo finally advised the green-antlered recruit. "I have it on good authority that Alvarez doesn't run a bunch of ragtag freebooters or some greasy-sack outfit that can't shoot straight."

"That reckless bastard fouled a fine nest down in Hermosillo," Grizz Bear took over. "Had him a gun-running setup until the federals run him across the border for welching on his bribes. Lately he's been ruling the roost in the Mojave, robbing prospectors and paymasters and such."

"I take your drift," young Jude said. "He knows dang well his fortunes depend on keeping the desert military outposts weak and low on supplies."

"Now you're whistling," Fargo said. "I've never locked horns with Alvarez before. But I've talked to reliable soldiers and lawmen who have. They all claim he's got a private army, well organized, well armed, and numbering up in the scores when he calls them all in."

And it seemed only logical to Fargo that a man like Pablo Alvarez would know exactly what this strange U.S. Army experiment, which included the gringo *famoso* Skye Fargo, meant if it succeeded: like the kid just said, it was the end of the Scorpion's criminal bonanza.

Fargo had fought men like the Scorpion before. Some, like their bloodthirsty leader, had learned brutal, casual killing in the charnel house of the 1846–47 war. Others hailed from around the Scorpion's hometown of La Cuesta. These competent killers were loyal to a ruthless savage who murdered the innocent as casually as he swatted at flies.

Grizz Bear shifted his attention to the dead Mexican. "You s'pose the beaners will want to bury him?"

"We'll all bury him," Jude spoke up, offended. "He's part of the expedition."

"He never bought *me* a beer," Grizz Bear noted. "So fuck him."

The wind suddenly whipped up, sand and grit assaulting

Fargo's face like buckshot. He tugged the brim of his hat lower and pulled his red bandanna up over his nose and mouth.

That body, Fargo reminded himself. It could be a lure. . . .

"Rider coming from camp," Jude said. "Looks like Juan Salazar."

Not even ten in the morning, Fargo thought, and the desert heat was already so thick it had weight on his shoulders and the back of his neck. Ragged parcels of cloud drifted slowly across a deep blue dome of sky. Again he studied the terrain they were about to cross. There was very little, beyond the river growth, but the occasional twisted yucca tree or tall, narrow cactus the local Indians called Spanish bayonets.

"Yeah, take a good gander, Trailsman," Grizz Bear cut into his thoughts. "You know 'er, boy, and so do I. That Mojave is hell turned inside out, and it just . . . don't . . . *stop.*"

The old salt glanced at Jude. "That's gospel truth, sprout. And *dry?* Why, there's stretches ahead of us so damn dry they got three-year-old fish that ain't learned to swim yet. This ain't like that ninety-mile stretch back in New Mex. Get set for a hell-buster. The consarn army will rue the day it sent soft-handed children and desk soldiers to stand in for men."

The kid puffed himself up and slapped the stock of his Sharps. Like the rest of the soldiers on this expedition he wore a mixture of civilian and military clothes.

"It's been rough country since we left San Antonio and it ain't whipped me," Jude boasted. "This desert coming up ain't nothing but more of the same. If them ugly camels can take it, so can I."

"Pup, them ships of the desert will shit on *all* our bones."

"Quit trying to scare the kid," Fargo cut in impatiently. "Jude, if a man learns the desert he needn't fear it. Besides, a man's got to die someplace. I'm not particular about the terrain."

Fargo paused to watch Juan Salazar trot closer on an army mule. The Mexican ranch hand had hired on back in San Antone. He was taciturn but civil, a good worker who kept to himself most of the time. But his habit of deliberately avoiding eye contact with others gave the constant impression he was a sneak thief.

Grizz Bear poked the corpse indifferently with the toe of his boot. "If it's Alvarez done this, you kallate he'll have the main gather with him?"

Fargo shook his head. "I don't know the man's tactics first-hand. But I'd guess he'll hold off at first—dust puffs give away big groups in the desert. I'd say he'll try to cold-deck us with just a few of his best killers—more stuff like with Lupe. But mainly I'm worried they'll try to kill the camels. There're no replacements, and it was a helluva deal to buy them and get them here."

He expelled a long sigh. "This is why I wanted to fight shy of the sand-dune country west of Fort Yuma. That's a bog-down stretch and we'd be fish in a barrel if well-hidden dry-gulchers opened up. Looks like they just followed us—"

Fargo's next word snagged in his throat when a rifle spoke its deadly piece from the nearby river bluff, shattering the hot stillness.

That first bullet snapped past Fargo's face and impacted only inches from his stallion, raising a gravel plume near the big horse's front hooves. The Ovaro reared up, nickering more in irritation than fright. Fargo let it go when the stallion began crow-hopping—the mount was bullet-trained and the shooter would have to earn his target.

"Hell, kid, you bolted down?" he snapped at Jude. "Quit gawking and kiss the deck!"

The other men had already covered down. Again, again, the repeating rifle cracked with a shattering clarity in the transparent desert air. The bullets, ricocheting from boulder to boulder all around them, sent off a screaming whine that especially agitated the horses and mules.

Had the hidden marksman blued his barrel Fargo would not likely have taken his next gamble. But exposed metal caught just enough sun to glint from a steep, rock-strewn sandbank rising up above the river.

Fargo's trouble-honed reflexes didn't wait for further confirmation. Using that glint as his fixed reference, Fargo rose to a kneeling-offhand position, worked the lever of the Henry repeater, and threw the rifle butt into his shoulder. The brass frame was hot from the sun when he laid his cheek against it and notched his bead, deadly lead still snapping past him so close it was personal.

"Let 'er rip!" Grizz Bear bellowed as Fargo methodically and rapidly set to work with his sixteen-shot Henry, holding a tight pattern with that momentary glint at its core.

Fargo was as surprised as everyone else when, all of a moment, a man came plunging down the steep, rocky slope of the sandbank.

He was only wounded and still alive at first—Fargo could hear him screaming as he slammed from rock to rock, plummeting downward toward the slack-jawed men. His rifle clattered along behind him like a faithful pet trying to catch up.

The four men advanced cautiously to examine the ambusher. Though his only gunshot wound was to the left knee, the battering tumble had killed the man before he quit rolling.

"Hell, I figured you to drill him right through the brainpan," Grizz Bear remarked, staring at the bruised and battered face and misshapen skull. "I ain't never seen this chili pep before. A-course, his face is messed up considerable so's a body can't be sure."

Fargo moved forward and brought the rifle back, an old Collier seven-shot revolving carbine that had been converted from touchhole to percussion. The sight had broken off in the tumble, but the weapon appeared serviceable. He bent over and removed a bandolier of bullets and percussion caps from the body. The man wore no sidearm.

Juan Salazar craned his neck to look past Grizz Bear. Fargo watched him stare at the corpse, much of the color draining from his copper skin. He looked like a man who had just been mule-kicked but not quite dropped.

"Santissima Maria," he whispered hoarsely, making the sign of the cross.

"You know him?" Fargo demanded.

Salazar turned in Fargo's direction but averted his eyes. He was a young man in his twenties and wore the leather *chivarra* pants of a Mexican cowboy.

"Yes, I know him," he replied. "His name is Roberto de Torreon de Salazar. The man you have just killed is my brother."